COLOR
OF
WINTER

AN INSPIRATIONAL NOVEL

Angela C. Griffiths

Unless otherwise indicated, all scripture quotations are taken from the King James Version of the Bible.

1st Printing

COLOR OF WINTER

ISBN 9798338571057

Copyright ©2024 by Angela C. Griffiths

Published by
Angela C. Griffiths

Dedications

I dedicate this book to all my single readers. To all my dedicated single readers with you in mind as I write this book. As I wrote these words, the Lord gave me this prayer for you while you wait for your soul mate. Lord teach me patience to wait to walk when you want me to walk. Teach me to run when you want me to run, guide my thoughts, guide my heart and my words, guide and direct my paths. Enable me to know who to connect with spiritually and who to love, who to give my heart and to grow with! Teach me to have that one-on-one vertical relationship with you first in all areas of my life. help me to find and fall in love with you, my first true love which is you! Then help guide me to that human love that will compliment me. But only you can and will complete me.

TABLE OF CONTENTS

Chapter 1
REMINISCING 1

Chapter 2
STARTING OVER 11

Chapter 3
THE RECOVERY PERIOD 18

Chapter 4
THE SURPRISE 26

Chapter 5
THE GOSSIP 33

Chapter 6
VACATION TO AFRICA 44

Chapter 7
LIFE THREATENING SITUATION 50

Chapter 8
STAGE OF HEALING 59

Chapter 9
HOME SWEET HOME...73

Chapter 10
THE BIRTH OF HER GRANDSON 90

Chapter 11

THE DATE 103

Chapter12

JALON'S BIRTHDAY 117

Chapter 13

PICNIC AT THE PARK...126

Chapter 14

CAROLINE'S UPCOMMING BIRTHDAY 132

Chapter 15

THE PLANS 149

Chapter 16

THE SELECTIONS...165

Chapter 17

THE RESERVATION..183

Chapter 18

COUNT DOWN 193

Chapter 19

THEIR SPECIAL DAY..200

Chapter 20

THEIR HONEYMOON 222

Chapter 21

RETURN TO THE SANCTUARY 233

"In The Middle of Your Difficulties

Lies Opportunity."

Albert Einstein

CHAPTER 1
REMINISCING

It was early in the morning as Caroline sat on her front porch. She looked up and noticed the changes in the leaves on the trees. The birds were chirping, singing wonderful love songs to each other. The air was brisk and cool as the sun peeked over the horizon. Caroline was in deep thought, reminiscing about her past, her present circumstances, and what the future held for the rest of her life.

Caroline had lived an accomplished life and had done well for herself. Once upon a time, she was married, but life had dealt her a hard hand, and suddenly she found herself in a desolate place. She now had to pick up the pieces of what was left. She was willing to start over, brushing herself off and moving on. She was a fighter, strong and full of love for life. But this time she knew there would be challenges. Isolated and alone, Caroline relied on herself with no friends, just a few associates. She moved to a new township, not by choice, but as a place to live until she could get herself together. Her son and daughter-in-law welcomed her with open arms and provided plenty of love and encouragement. When she arrived in the strange town, it was hard for Caroline. She cried many nights as she reminisced about what she had and had lost. She tried to make sense of what had happened.

She thought to herself, "No husband, no business, job, no money, and no place to call my own." Caroline asked herself, "How did I get here?" Wondering about the circumstances she found herself in, she pondered, "What did I do wrong? What is next, and where do I go from here?" As she pondered these questions, a scripture verse came to her memory. One she had read in the past. Though she could not remember where it came from or quote it exactly, it said, "Do not look on the things of your past. Do not think about them because I, the Lord, will do a new thing and you will know when it happens." Then she heard a still, small still voice saying, "Be encouraged, even though you are in a desolate place, my daughter."

As that scripture verse came to her mind, she remembered that before she had anything or became accomplished, it was the Lord who had brought her there. She knew if He had brought her out before, then, He would bring her out once again. The town was very small. Everyone knew each other. It was very isolated and not well-developed. During the day, she would read her daily words. She would see one or two strangers as they passed by her gate and say "Hello". In the evening hours, the only sounds of life were a few local traffic noises from people heading home from work and the small park across the way where a few children would come out and play when their parents brought them out. You could hear their laughter as they played. Other than the children, there was the dreaded sound of the train that passed by every so often. It was loud enough to wake the dead.

As the days went by, the colors of winter started to show. The evenings became colder, the days shorter, and the nights longer. "Dear Lord," she cried, "Get me through this. Do not let me lose my mind." The loneliness and isolation started to set in as Caroline scrambled to find things to do during the days and evenings to occupy her time. She would go to the local library just within walking distance of the house during the days to pick out good books to take home and read. She would also use the internet to search for work and pick up a few good movies to watch in the evenings to prevent boredom from setting in.

Eventually, she found a local church close to where she lived in the next town over. They had transportation services to pick her up for service on Wednesday's and Sunday's. She was incredibly happy and thankful because it was a blessing in disguise. She did not have to bother her son and daughter-in-law for a ride to the church. It also gave her an opportunity to get out of the house, to be uplifted, and inspired by the church services. It gave her a chance to meet new people and socialize with them.

She was so happy to get out of the house until she would get dressed and ready at least one hour before they picked her up for services. They were always on time. A young man named Jalon was the one who drove the van and picked her up. He was a nice gentleman, always polite, respectful, and with a smile. At the stop, he would get out of the van, open the door, and put down the footstool so she could climb in. As she entered, he would gently close the door behind her as she sat down. Then he would continue to pick up the rest of the members and head to the church. They would arrive just in time for the service to start. Caroline would find a seat in the third row and enjoyed the praise and worship service. The church had many activities including a women's ministry on Tuesday nights, a youth ministry on Thursday nights, and a singles ministry on Friday nights.

As she got acclimated to the new church and its activities, she started to meet new people and exchange phone numbers with a few church members. On Saturdays, Caroline would get together with her new friends and go out on the town to the movies, skating, bowling, sightseeing, shopping, or just out to a restaurant for dinner or lunch. On these days Caroline did not go out to seek employment. She would occupy her time by going over to the small park across from the house where she stayed. There, she would draw, paint, and sometimes write poems. These were hobbies and pastimes she had enjoyed for many years. She had not drawn or painted in years until now. She had been so busy that she never took the time to do the things she enjoyed. Now she enjoyed doing them again.

As she spent time alone in the park, she observed the beauty of God's nature in the trees as the colors of the leaves changed from green to the beautiful fall colors of red, orange, yellow, gold, burgundy, brown, green, and a tinge of pink. She enjoyed the fresh, crisp air and the warm sunshine on her skin.

As she looked around, she realized that things could have been worse in her situation. She wept, then shortly after, thanked God for where she was. She realized that some people were in worse situations than she was. She looked across the way and saw a homeless couple sitting on a bench with bags in a shopping cart. They were talking and having a hot dog and a soda. Her heart was filled with empathy and compassion towards them. This made her realize it could have been her sitting in their position. She prayed for them but did not have any money to offer, just her love. This opened her eyes even more to be thankful to the Lord for what she had. As she looked up to the heavens, she cried once again, not for sorrow but for joy for where she was, even though she did not like the situation. She started to pray again, looking to the heavens after seeing the couple.

Caroline said, "Lord, I thank you once again for providing me with shelter, food, clothing, and most of all, life, and health. I thank you for keeping me in my right mind, for allowing me to think clearly. I love you. Let me not take you or anything you do for me for granted, even the simplest things we often overlook, such as walking, speaking, breathing, and using our hands and feet, while others have lost the use of their body parts and depend on others for daily assistance. Once again, Lord, I pray not to take you or these blessings for granted."

Caroline now had a greater sense of awareness and appreciation. As she continued to pray, she wept. She said, "Even though at times I do not understand, help me. I know that I am here and reconnected to you again. Show me the way, show me how I can help in the church. Where do you want to use me to be a blessing to your people? For the glory of your name, amen. Thank you, Lord, for hearing my prayer!" As she prayed, she felt a peace and joy in her spirit that she had never experienced before since moving to the new town.

As she continued to draw and paint, she observed the birds chirping in the trees, the clear blue skies, and the sunshine, marveling at the majesty and wonders of God's handiwork. As she drew and painted, she continued to contemplate her life. She started to realize one of the reasons she ended up in her current state: she had left her first love, God. She had walked away from serving and thanking Him years ago when life was good. When things in her life were beautiful, she eventually stopped spending time with Him in His word. She stopped praying and was less thankful for what she had. Gradually, things started to spiral out of control. First, her finances dwindled; afterward, she lost several business contracts. Eventually, the doors of her business closed. The money she had saved in the bank and other investments went bad due to some poor investments.

Then her health started to fail due to the stress of her business failure and financial losses. Her husband began having affairs and was unfaithful to her. Infidelity crept in, and they would argue constantly until he finally said, "I want out. This is not working. I am not happy with you anymore." Then he packed his bags and left, taking almost everything that was left in their bank account. Whatever investments remained had to be sold and split evenly. Eventually, he filed for divorce. The home she had built from the ground up became a burden. It was too expensive for her to afford, so she sold it at a low price to prevent foreclosure. Caroline was broken-hearted and alone. As she looked back on how things had been, she realized it had been a gradual decline, one event after another, until everything was gone. She knew the exact reasons why she had lost everything and was in her current situation. She felt embarrassed, ashamed, and guilty. She had to put away her selfish pride and talk with the Lord, admitting her failure to Him. She knew it was not God's fault; He had never left her, but she had left Him. She had used the material things she possessed as "idols" until they were all gone. Then she realized that things would come and go, but God would never leave. She admitted to herself that she should serve the Creator, and He would continually supply her needs. She also realized that God would break you, but He will bless you. God never uses anything until He breaks it, and she was broken so He could use her for His purpose.

This was when reality set in. She needed to start seeking and serving God wholeheartedly and be obedient to Him in all areas of her life. She realized she needed to put Him first in everything she did and acknowledge Him so that He could guide and direct her footsteps from that time forward. It was a hard pill to swallow, but she knew she had to be honest with herself and with God.

Shortly after crying out to the Lord, she asked, "Dear Lord, why am I here? What is it you would like for me to do?" A few weeks later, she felt inspired to talk with the pastor about helping singles and couples interested in starting their own businesses as she was already an experienced businesswoman. The pastor agreed, allowing her to teach the congregation members who were interested in stepping out on faith to start their own businesses or return to school to further their business education. Many people signed up to join the class. [OBJ]

Caroline now felt as if she belonged and found her purpose. It was to help people in the church further their goals. She was happy and excited about what she was about to do. Once the new class started, more people signed up for the next upcoming class. She was extremely excited about doing the work of God, teaching, and advising on business. The class grew, and now people were becoming more independent and self-sufficient, able to pay for their tithes and offerings because most had finally found their purpose after completing the class.

Caroline began spending more personal time getting closer to and more acquainted with the Lord. She stopped complaining and prayed more, patiently waiting for answers and directions. Her prayers became more transparent and targeted specific areas of her life and family that needed healing and deliverance. These prayers were unselfish; she even started to pray for the church ministry, the pastor, and her ex-husband. She felt excited and happy, as though her life finally had purpose and direction.

Eventually, Caroline found work in a field she enjoyed. Soon after, she was able to buy a car. She thanked God for her renewed independence, as she could now get around on her own without relying on anyone for a ride. She no longer needed to ride in the church van on Sundays. Instead, she could pick up a few people on her way to church, and she was elated. She missed speaking with the nice, polite gentleman, Jalon, but they periodically saw each other at church, depending on their seating locations. Sometimes, they ran into each other at the end of the service or greeted each other during the service.

"Great things happen to those who don't stop believing, trying, learning, and being grateful."

Roy T. Bennett

CHAPTER 2
STARTING OVER

The Lord began to bless Caroline exponentially, and she started looking for a new home nearby. After a few months, she moved into her new place. She held a home blessing celebration and invited her pastor, along with a few new friends and associates from the church. It was a Saturday evening, and they had a wonderful time. They drank, laughed, listened to soft, relaxing music, and some danced throughout the evening. Everyone was astonished by how big and beautiful the home was and the amazing price she paid for it. Most said she was certainly blessed, and some remarked, "God has favored you, Caroline." They talked and laughed until the party ended.

As Caroline said goodnight to her guests and reminisced about their conversations, she realized how truly blessed she was. The Lord had restored everything she had lost in a short period of time. She understood that this was because of her obedience and humility in serving God with her whole heart and because she had found His purpose for her predestined many years ago. Now she was happy.

She sat and drank a cup of coffee, worshipping the Lord in her heart for His goodness and grace in her life. She felt genuinely happy and fulfilled, experiencing joy and peace like never before. Her new house was light, bright, and open. It was in a family neighborhood, surrounded by many families, unlike the isolated and desolate place she lived in before with her son and daughter-in-law. She could now breathe a sigh of relief from the depressing and lonely feeling she had while living there.

Caroline began shopping for furnishings that suited her taste, decorating the entire house one room at a time. It became beautiful, and she was so happy to have her own place once again. She thanked God for her own transportation, her new home, and everything else falling into place as the Lord continued to bless her.

One day, as Caroline was on her way to work, she felt extremely uncomfortable in her spirit. She was in a hurry, and the time allotted that day did not allow her to get into her studies and the Word, as she usually did every morning. Normally, she would turn on the radio and listen to her favorite Christian station as she drove to work, but for some reason, the radio station seemed to be a bit off-tune and fuzzy. So, while waiting at a red light, she corrected the tuning. Out of nowhere, a drunk driver ran through the red light and hit her car. It spun out of control. Poor Caroline did not know what had happened. Her car was totaled, and she was in and out of consciousness. When she awoke, her son and daughter-in-law were at her bedside. It was her boss who had called her son, reporting that she did not show up for work and that it was not like Caroline not to show up or call in for work. It was shortly after someone from the accident scene found and used her phone and called her son. They did not leave their name, just a message, where the accident took place, and the hospital she was going to. The air ambulance came and took her to the hospital because it was a serious car accident. When her son arrived at the hospital, he was very worried and overwhelmed. His wife asked for her purse, found her phone, and immediately called Caroline's pastor at the church she attended for prayers on her behalf. That evening, they gathered together at the church and prayed for her safety and life because Caroline had to have immediate surgery. A short while later, her pastor arrived at the hospital to comfort and pray for Caroline, her son, and daughter-in-law, encourage them, and give them an uplifting word before she went in for surgery. The surgery lasted three to four hours because she fractured her left arm and had a few cuts and bruises on her face, chest, and legs. The doctor who performed the surgery came and spoke with her son and daughter-in-law. He told them the surgery was successful and that it was a miracle her life was spared. Based on the condition of the car, it was a miracle she did not sustain more injuries than what she had sustained. Her son and daughter-in- law thanked the doctor for his skillful hands, and he replied, "It was the Lord who was watching over your mother." As soon as he heard the statement, tears started to flow from his eyes, but it was tears of joy. His mom was alive, and what the doctor said echoed in his spirit and heart. It was a miracle; it was a miracle her life was spared, and he remembered telling the doctor it was because of the Lord. He now realized it was truly the Lord who was by her side watching over her. Then he started to realize how short life is and how fragile she was; she could have been swept away and gone to the other side to be with the Lord. He now started to see that if the Lord had taken his mom. At this moment, he started also to examine and evaluate his own life and relationships with the Lord, realizing he was not where he should be. At that time, he asked the pastor how and what he needed to do to recommit his life to God because all he did was work, and it seemed as if something was missing and there was more to life than just work. What happened to his mom was a wake-up call. He cried as he spoke with the pastor; it took this moment for him to realize how short and precious life is. As the pastor explained to him that it is good but most times it has to take tragedy for people or families to wake up and realize the reality of life, he continued to speak with the pastor. He asked the question, "Why? Why? Why would God let an accident like this happen that almost took her life? She is a good woman and one who is dedicated to serving the Lord. Why?" As the pastor composed himself and answered the questions, he told him that tragedy happens in life, but it is not God who wants to take her life; it's the enemy, the devil, who wants to take her prematurely. It is the devil who is angry because your mom is dedicated to God's will and work. He is the one who wanted to stop her from doing more good work. As you can see, she is helping people that want to stay in the same negative positions and bad situations they are in. So, he is mad and angry and tried to kill her, but it was God's angels that encamped around her to protect her from death. It is because it was not her time; God was not ready for her; there is yet more work for her to do for God's kingdom.

He cried more as the pastor stated those words, and it echoed once again in his ears and heart. But as he heard these comforting words, he also realized that if it were not for this tragedy, he probably would not have rededicated his life to God at this time. He thanked the pastor with a handshake and embraced him with a hug. As the pastor got ready to leave and go home, he reassured him that all is well and that "everything is going to be okay." He told him to call him if he needed to talk, and he said goodbye. A short while later, they brought Caroline out of surgery to the recovery room. They stayed the night by her side each day until she was conscious because she was disoriented and was fading in and out of consciousness. When Caroline awoke three days later and saw her son and daughter-in-law at her bedside, she was finally able to talk and realized she was in the hospital. She asked, "Why am I here?" Then her daughter-in-law and son answered and told her she had a bad accident and had been in the hospital for a few days. They cried as her son and daughter-in-law embraced her and told her how much he loved her. He was fearful when he heard the news and saw the condition she was in; he thought he was going to lose her. She cried when she heard and saw the cast on her arm and the cuts and bruises on her body. They told her that her pastor was there for a while and that they had been praying for her. She knew the Lord spared her life. As she became more conscious, stable, and stronger each day, the pastor would stop by periodically to pray and encourage her. Some of her church family and friends stopped by to cheer her up, wishing her well and a speedy recovery, giving her cards, balloons, and flowers. The pastor was very sad to see her in the condition she was, and he offered her his help and if she needed anything when she was discharged from the hospital. He gave her his phone number just in case. They talked for a while and then prayed once again, encouraging her before he left the hospital and headed home.

"Happiness is not by chance

but by choice"

John Rohn

CHAPTER 3

THE RECOVERY PERIOD

A week later, Caroline was discharged from the hospital and sent home. She had help at home for a few weeks followed by therapy. She had many visitors regularly offering their help, and she was grateful and appreciative. Her daughter-in-law and son would stop by daily to prepare meals for her, shop, wash, and clean the house. She also had visits from Jalon periodically, and he would drop off food she had a taste for and desired. He would also make himself available to take her to her doctor's appointments because she was unable to drive with the cast on her arm. Eventually, the cuts healed, and the bruises went away.

During the healing process at home, Caroline decided to work from home instead of returning to the office. She eventually saved enough money, resigned from her job, and started her own business working from home. Caroline's business flourished and expanded quickly, growing to the point where she needed to hire help. The church family would often call to check on her and offer their services if needed. Meanwhile, at the church, Jalon periodically drove the church bus on an as needed or emergency basis when no one else was available to pick up people for services. He was completing his theological studies to become a pastor, so he would sit and observe his pastor. On some Sundays and Wednesday night Bible study services, he would conduct the services. Eventually, he told Caroline about it, and she was very happy and excited for him. He was pleased to see her enthusiasm.

Weeks after the accident, Caroline was doing well, feeling much better and stronger. She started to venture back to the church, but she was still unable to drive on her own, so she took the church bus. Jalon offered to pick her up and drop her at home after services.

One evening after service, he nervously asked Caroline if she would accompany him to stop and have a bite to eat because he was hungry and had not eaten much all day. She pleasantly accepted but was not very hungry because she had eaten supper before coming out to Bible study services. She replied to Jalon, "That is not good for you to walk around all day on an empty stomach!" He acknowledged that she was right. Caroline suggested that he take a cup of hot tea first before ordering and eating a heavy meal. He was elated by the suggestion, saw wisdom in what she said, and saw the caring side of her. As they waited for the waitress to come and take their orders, they talked about their day. Finally, the waitress arrived and took their orders, and a short while later brought a large pot of hot tea. As he sipped on it, he started to feel much better. Caroline ordered only a salad and a large raspberry iced tea so that Jalon did not feel insulted by her not ordering anything.

Jalon said, "Is that all you are ordering? You eat very little." With a smile on his face, Caroline replied, "Remember I told you I was not very hungry because I had eaten before coming out to the service. I did not want to embarrass you by not ordering anything! I try to be sensitive to people's feelings." Then Jalon shook his head and said, "I understand," as he took note of her.

While they waited to be served, they continued to talk and laugh throughout the evening. Caroline said, "Although you are a serious man when it comes to the work of the Lord, outside of that, you are a true comedian. I enjoy laughter after all I have been through." Jalon responded, "I enjoy making and seeing others laugh and be happy. Even though we are Christians, that does not mean we should always be serious. There is a time and a place for everything, and the Lord also wants us to be happy." She replied, "I certainly agree with you on that!"

Finally, the waitress arrived with their orders. Jalon took Caroline's hands and initiated prayers by blessing their food. They ate and ended the evening by taking Caroline home. Once again, he politely opened the car door for Caroline and escorted her to her front door and opened it for her because, being left-handed with the cast, it was difficult for her to open the door. As they said goodnight, Caroline told Jalon that she would call him later when he got home. "Drive safely getting home," she stated, "Thanks again and have a good night." She waved and slowly closed the door once he walked and entered his vehicle. He had a smile on his face, thinking about her gestures and how considerate she was by saying she would call and check on him to make sure he made it home safely. No other woman had ever said or done that for him before. As he meditated on what she said, he thought to himself, "This woman is different!"

Caroline waited about an hour and then called Jalon to say goodnight and make sure he made it home safely. She did exactly what she had told him she would. He was not surprised she called because he discerned, she was a woman of her word. They spoke for a short period of time and then said goodnight. A few weeks later, the doctor gave Caroline the okay and removed the cast from her arm. He told her the setting and healing process went well, and her arm looked great. She was now able to return to her routine daily activities but needed a few more therapy treatments. It was up to her how she felt after therapy if she wanted to continue. Caroline was very happy the cast was removed. She was less constricted and now able to move her fingers without restrictions. She had no pain, swelling, or discoloration. She was very happy to be independent and able to drive herself once again. She called Jalon and told him the good news. He was very happy, and so was she. Now she was able to start working at the church again, and her new home business was blossoming. It was doing very well, and she was proud, happy, and thankful to God. Her pastor and church family were happy to see her return to what she loved. Her son, now on a routine basis, and his family were grateful and appreciative to the Lord for sparing his mother's life and her recovery.

Jalon was now doing sermons periodically as his pastor requested for him to exercise his skills, gain experience, and build confidence as he prepared to go out on his own. A few months later, Jalon pondered over the evening they went out to eat and how Caroline was so mindful and caring, making sure he made it home safely and making a follow-up call. They had spoken since then, but casually, greeting each other as they passed by in church. But lately, Jalon's mind had been on Caroline, and he did not know how to talk to her about how he really felt. This was different.

Caroline was of fair complexion, medium-built, 5'5", beautiful, very mature, intelligent, and filled with the Spirit. She was humble but feisty, and she took the work of the Lord seriously. Because of her looks and personality, most men were intimidated by her, and she dressed very classy and elegant. Even in the most casual outfit, she wore it well. Jalon, on the other hand, was tall, 6'3", medium-built, mocha complexion, and very handsome. He was also very mature, intelligent, and spiritual. He also took the Lord's work very seriously and was a sharp and classy dresser. Very humble, soft-spoken, and respectful. Another few weeks went by, and it was driving Jalon mad seeing Caroline go by week after week in church without being able to say a word.

The following Sunday after service, Jalon finally made up his mind. With that burning desire in his heart to speak with Caroline, he approached her as she was on her way out the door. "Hello," he said, and she stopped abruptly when he mentioned her name. She looked towards him as he smiled. "How are you?" he asked. "How are you feeling now that it's been a few weeks since the doctor removed the cast?" She stretched out her arm and showed him it was completely healed, with only a few minimal scars. She replied, "I am doing fine, thank you for asking!" They chatted for a little while, and as she said goodbye, he gently interrupted her and said, "Caroline, are you in a hurry?" She answered, "No." Surmising he wanted to ask her something else, she softly said, "Is there something else I can do for you?" Jalon was very relieved because she made it easier for him to ask the questions he wanted to ask. He replied, "If you would do me the honor and are not in a hurry, I would like to speak with you in person privately." "Okay," she replied. Then he asked if she was hungry. "Have you eaten, or do you have plans to go home and eat?" he asked. She said, "I was planning to go home and warm up some leftovers I made yesterday!" He then said, "Would you mind if we talk at the local restaurant downtown while we have a bite to eat?" She replied, "Certainly," wondering what he wanted to talk about that they could not have talked about over the phone. He said, "Okay, that's the plan. Follow me." She headed towards her car, and she did too, and she followed him to the restaurant. He quickly parked his car, got out, and met her by her car, opening the car door for her. He gently held her hand as she stood up and shut the door behind her. "A true gentleman," she said to herself and thanked Jalon. Very few men still have the courtesy to continue to be kind, respectful, and courteous, as she gave him a smile.

"Love is a tender touch, that ignites
the sparks of one's heart"
Angela C. Griffiths

CHAPTER 4

THE SURPRISE

As they walked towards the restaurant, Jalon seemed nervous. "Are you okay?" Caroline asked. He replied, "I am fine." As they entered the restaurant, the hostess met them and seated them at a table close to the window. The sun was shining, and it was a beautiful Sunday afternoon. The weather was perfect. The waitress asked, "What would you like to drink?" Caroline ordered strawberry iced tea, and he ordered lemonade. "It is a perfect day for a lemonade," he said as he tried to calm down, while Caroline patiently waited for him to say what was on his mind.

Jalon said to Caroline, "Thank you for coming out on such short notice." She replied, "No trouble at all, thank you! All I was planning to do was go home, relax, watch some television, and since it is a nice day, sit outside and possibly do some reading for a while. I welcome the change." Finally, Jalon said, "I hope I do not sound too intrusive. I know we talk on the phone sometimes, and while you were unable to drive, I picked you up for church services. I wanted to know if there is anyone special in your life. What do I mean, as he stuttered, a close friend or possibly a relationship?" He was so nervous that perspiration ran down from his forehead to his chin, and he took his handkerchief and wiped it away.

Caroline responded, "No, there is no one interested or in my life." She was calm, cool, and collected, but deep down, she was a bit nervous inside, wondering, "Wow! I was not expecting this." Jalon was happy. He had a smile on his face and was relieved after asking her the questions that had been weighing heavily on his heart. Because Caroline responded with no, he again wiped the sweat away from his forehead. Jalon said, "I just had to ask to make sure I am not intruding. Now that the air has been cleared, I just wanted to let you know that a few months ago, the last time we stopped and had something to eat, you said something that has held on to my heart. To make things more complicated, I miss picking you up for church services. I enjoyed doing it, and I miss seeing you."

Caroline was very surprised by his statement. "What are you trying to say?" she asked. Jalon replied, "Caroline, if you do not mind, I would like to ask you out on a 'date.' I am not sure if you are interested in taking our friendship or even a relationship at this time! You are a very interesting, intelligent, and beautiful woman. I would like to get the chance to get to know you better."

Caroline was speechless and surprised, blushing before she could speak and answer his question. Jalon was nervously waiting for her answer, hoping it would not be no. Caroline responded, "I had no

27

idea you felt this way. I did not know you were secretly admiring me." He responded, "I was not really admiring you! It just snuck up on me that evening when we stopped at that restaurant after the Bible study services." As he was speaking, they both smiled at each other, and he continued, "I saw something in you that I had never seen before in any woman. I saw a side of you that is very rare, a caring side. No one has ever taken such an interest in me like this before, and that stayed with me. I saw that you were quite different from other women, admirable and special."

Caroline said, "Thank you! That is just the way I have been all my life." Jalon shook his head and said, "Wow!" Finally, she said, "This was unexpected. I was not planning to engage in a relationship, but I did ask the Lord to send me good friends." As she looked into his brownish-gray eyes, she saw sadness and disappointment. She clarified her statement by saying, "I am not saying no to going out with you. We will go out on some dates, and as time goes on, the friendship may develop into something more, but I do not want to rush into a relationship right away. I believe a relationship should start off as being friends."

Jalon smiled and agreed with her statement. As they continued to speak, the waitress stopped by and took their orders. Shortly after, the server brought their water, more drinks, and appetizers. As they sipped on their drinks and nibbled on their appetizers, they continued to talk. Meanwhile, in Caroline's heart, she was very happy because she had secretly admired Jalon's demeanor, kindness, patience, and humility. The pleasantness of him was very attractive to Caroline, and she was pleased that he admired her enough to ask her out on a date. Once again, she was very surprised. She said to herself, "Of all the women in the church and those elsewhere, he found interest in me." Caroline was still a bit insecure, and her self-esteem was a bit low, but she was getting stronger. This insecurity stemmed from the way her ex-husband had treated her. But she knew as time passed by, she would be healed by God's grace. Caroline now believed God had answered her prayers. It seemed as if Jalon was that wonderful guy the Lord had sent her way. He was one of the meekest people you could meet and be around. Then he called her name and said, "Caroline, Caroline, are you okay? Have you heard anything I said?" She said, "Yes, I did. Forgive me if I seem to be in a daze. I was still amazed about all of this." Jalon asked, "Why?" She replied, "After all that I have been through, I never expected you or anyone else at this time to show any interest in me." Jalon said, "What?" She repeated, "I never thought anyone would show interest in me." He said, "I cannot believe I am hearing you correctly." She said, "Yes, you are!" He responded, "Such an attractive, intelligent, and beautiful woman such as yourself!" She said, "Oh, you do not know anything about me or my life story." Jalon responded, "A true man knows quality when he sees it. He knows a humble, honest, and real woman of God when he sees her. So, whatever your story is, it won't change my mind either way! To be honest, if you want to talk about your past, I will listen. But to be honest, I am not interested because whoever you had in the past for a husband was a fool to let you go! He did not know what he wanted, and he did not know what was good. I know it is not good to judge a book before reading it, but I can also say this: just in the short period of time I spent with you, as we went back and forth to church and communicated on the phone, what the Lord showed me in my spirit, I can truly say you are a good person. Whoever was in your life and let you go, it's his loss. Evidently, he did not deserve you, and the Lord sees that you deserve better."

Caroline heard everything that came out of Jalon's mouth. She was pleasantly surprised and uplifted in her spirit. She did not feel as if he was saying it to make her feel good, to make a good impression, or for any ulterior motives. She felt it was genuinely from the heart. Caroline responded gracefully with a simple thank you and a smile and was very emotional. Jalon then said, "I can see we will have a great friendship and a wonderful time together." She replied, "I believe so!" As soon as they said that the main course of their meal arrived. The server said, "Soup for both," then said, "Lobster soufflé truffles in butter sauce, with white rice and broccoli," and placed it in front of Jalon. Caroline said, "Oh, that looks and smells great." Jalon replied, "It is good. I had it before. I love seafood," he exclaimed! Caroline responded, "I do too." The server brought Caroline her plate with scallops and shrimp in cream butter sauce with a touch of lemon, served with baked potatoes and baby cabbage stalks. Jalon said, "Now that looks great. I never had that before." The server refilled their drinks and said, "Bon appétit, enjoy!" Then she asked, "Is there anything else you need?" They both shook their heads no because they were ready to eat. Jalon prayed and blessed the food, and they dug in. While they ate, they talked and complimented the menus they had chosen. They were both well-flavored and satisfied.

Caroline said to Jalon, "You seem to be such an honest, caring, and kind person, and an extremely attractive man yourself. Have you ever been married or had any children? And if so, why are you single and unattached?" Jalon said, "I have never been married and have no children. The reason for this is I was more focused on my studies, and I was not in any rush to get into a relationship. I am a very picky person when it comes to certain things. I am also very observant and like to take my time, especially when it comes to relationships and who I get involved with. I was not really ready for a relationship or even friendship until I spent time with you. I saw how beautiful you are, and when I say beautiful, I am talking about your heart, characteristics, intellect, and mind. After you got better and I was not able to pick you up anymore, I missed you. I am just being honest. I have never been around anyone in such a short period of time and felt this.

"Love can be gentle and uplifting, but when lost can be a painful deep dark valley"
Angela C. Griffiths

CHAPTER 5
THE GOSSIP

It was now Sunday, and she was excitedly anticipating talking with him. When she entered the sanctuary, she was very happy and excited to see everyone. However, while she waited in the church hall to be seated, she overheard two women gossiping about Jalon. They did not see Caroline, and she couldn't help but listen to what they were saying. They said, "Did you know Jalon has two children? They are twins from a past relationship he had, and he never took care of them. He abandoned them and the children's mother after he promised to marry her." To Caroline, this seemed like a dream and a conspiracy of lies made up to hurt her. Her heart dropped, and sadness overtook her. She was hurt by the jealousy and hate in their hearts because they knew she and Jalon were friends and were getting close in their relationship outside of the church. She was very anxious and unable to listen to the sermon as the pastor preached the word. Sticking by the pastor's side was Jalon! When the service was called to order, he spoke quietly and humbly, while Caroline's mind raced with questions and thoughts about what she had heard. She sat quietly, trying her best to be attentive and receptive to the service. Some of her fellow brothers and sisters of the church greeted her as they passed by to be seated, but she was in a daze and was not aware of their acknowledgment. She prayed to the Lord, asking Him to quiet her mind and heart so she could focus on the word and to remove the distractions from her mind. However, it was hard to focus based on all she had heard, and she hoped it was not true. She prayed the service would be over soon so that she could confront him with what she just heard.

Finally, the service ended with the benediction, and Jalon was the one called on to give the final benediction. As the last word was spoken, it seemed like forever to Caroline. She got up quickly and headed towards the door, but most of the congregation stopped her by embracing her with a hug. They were happy to see her back with a total commitment to the church and doing what she does best: helping people. What now seemed like a positive, hopeful, and trustworthy friendship leading in the right direction seemed to be spiraling into something of the past in her mind. As she ran out of the church towards her car, Jalon tried to get her attention, but she was in a hurry and very upset about what she had heard. She did not want to converse with him at that time; she was overwhelmed with anxiety and wanted to run home and calm down before speaking with him. Jalon knew it was not like Caroline to run out on him after church like that. He knew something was wrong because she would normally greet him and talk to him for a while, but this time she left without saying a word. It was then Jalon knew something was wrong, and he needed to find out what was upsetting Caroline so much that she left without saying goodbye.

He tried calling her on her phone, but it was still off from the church service, and it went straight to voicemail. He did not leave a message, figuring he would give her some time to turn the phone on and he would call back and talk to her in person. After a while, he tried again, but there was no answer, and once again it went straight to voicemail. Now he was a bit worried and hoped nothing had happened to her. He finally left a message on her voicemail, hoping she would return his call, but she never did. He stopped by her home, but she was not there. She had taken a long drive out of town to clear her mind, but the decisions of her past seemed to be haunting her based on that conversation she overheard from those two women at the church gossiping. The enemy seemed to be bringing back some of her past experiences and tormenting her mind about falling in love again, making her believe it would only end up as a failure like in her past. She tried to drown out the negative noise and voices trying to attach themselves to her psyche and emotions, but they seemed louder than ever before. She fought back and rebuked them. She was very angry, but the voices continued to return periodically, taunting her. She would try to block them out by turning up the music, but that only helped for a moment. She continued to drive, and by the time she realized it, she had driven over three hours without stopping. When she finally did stop, it was at a local restaurant to eat because she was hungry and had not eaten all day. She finally remembered that her phone was off and turned it on, seeing that there were missed calls and voicemail waiting.

She ignored listening to them and sat down to order something to eat. At this time, she was much calmer and thought about what to say to Jalon and how to approach him the next time she saw him because she wanted to speak with him face-to-face and look him in the eyes. After she finished eating, she continued driving a short distance until she located a beautiful park with a pond, a small waterfall, ducks swimming, and children playing nearby in a pool. She thought to herself, "This is just the thing I need to clear my mind." So, she pulled out her paper and pen and started to write. It was a perfect day to write, she thought, but once again her mind and thoughts were geared back to what was said in the morning at church by the gossipers. She started to write down questions to ask Jalon, hoping the questions she was writing down were not true because it would hurt her so much. She would be devastated and did not know how to take it. Again, her mind was flooded with negative thoughts. She was scared and very afraid to lose one of the closest friends she had since she arrived in the area. It was now very late as she headed back home. The phone rang several times, but she refused to answer, saddened and disappointed. She refused to talk to anyone. She avoided any contact with anyone for a few days and refused to return any phone calls.

Eventually, one evening Jalon showed up at her door, and now Caroline had to confront what she had been trying to avoid. As she opened the door, Jalon said, "Caroline! Are you okay? I was so worried about you. I tried calling, but you did not pick up the phone or return my calls. I did stop by on several occasions, but no one was home. On Sunday after church, I tried to get your attention, but you ran out so quickly I was unable to. What is wrong? Did I do something to upset you?" Caroline paused for a moment because she did not want to come off with an angry tone or demeanor or get more anxious than before. She pulled out the questions she wrote down a few days ago and handed them over to him. He read them with a look on his face, and as he answered, his voice changed with nervousness. "Yes," he said, and Caroline's heart dropped. Then he also said, "No." Now she was totally confused, emotional, and upset. She was hurt, angry, and not able to contain herself. She blurted out, "Jalon, you lied to me. Why would you hide all these things from me? I trusted you, knowing the circumstances of my past." Caroline was so hurt she burst into tears. Jalon tried to console and hold her as he tried to explain, but she was upset and very emotional. He couldn't speak for her to listen. He was also emotional and was hurting to see her hurting. He tried to let her know that he was sorry and did not mean to hurt her, but she continued to cry. He tried to console her again, but she refused and cried even more. She said, "All this time we have spent together, I told you the truth. Why couldn't you have been truthful and honest with me?"

Relationships are based on truth, trust, and honesty, not lies. Communication is key in any true friendship or relationship. You are a man of God! You know these things. You know my past. Why would you use lies to hurt me and destroy our friendship? You know if you had just opened and told me the truth, I would have understood. I would have listened and would not have judged you! And all he could do at this time was just listen because she was hurting so much. But is this the way I had to find out the truth? By hearing gossip from the gossipers of the church? You know I hate these things. But standing by and hearing these women whispering about you, I could not help myself but listen when your name was called. After hearing, I was hoping it was all a lie. Why, she asked. Why would you destroy our friendship like this? He tried once again to explain the best way he knew how, but she was too upset to listen and refused to be consoled. At this time, all her past hurts and bad memories came rushing back into her mind and tormented her. She felt it was enough to drive anyone to the asylum. Poor Jalon did not have a word to say. He was humbled and quiet, listening to Caroline speak and cry. He could not take it anymore. He tried consoling her once again, but she pushed him away. So, he kindly excused himself and told her that when she was calmer, they would try and talk another time. He did not want to leave her in the state of mind she was in, but it was best as he shut the door behind him. He was hurt and upset emotionally for her. He said to himself, "I truly wanted to stay by her side, but the more I tried, the more she got upset, so it was best for me to leave." She cried even more after he left, but Jalon was also hurting because he was not able to talk or console her. He felt bad, as if he had failed her. After all, it was his mistake that brought this on. As he closed the door behind him and walked away towards his car, he cried because he truly loved Caroline. Seeing the suffering and pain he caused her by not exposing the truth of his past hurt him and the woman he loved. She did not know what to do at this time but pray for forgiveness and healing, especially for Caroline.

He stayed for a while as he sat outside in his car, but he could still hear her crying and weeping. That hurt him even more. He did not know what to do but cry and reluctantly drove away slowly and went by a friend of his to talk and release his emotions. He tried calling Caroline, but she was too distraught to answer. It was no use. Jalon talked with his friend until the breaking of dawn. He told his friend he was not trying to hide anything from his past because he thought it was insignificant. But he realized now that it was significant to Caroline. It hurt him so much that he cried on his friend's shoulder because he truly loved Caroline and did not realize how much until now. He stated, "She is a good woman, a very kind and special person, the kind that is very rare to find. I hope I did not lose her friendship because of my selfish behavior. I truly hurt her by not telling her the complete truth." His friend consoled him, and then he said goodbye and went away. Early that morning when he got home, he was not able to sleep. His heart and mind were on Caroline and the state she was in when he left her the night before. She was distraught, and he was more concerned because she refused to answer the phone.

Caroline, too, was not able to sleep. She cried all night because she trusted Jalon and felt he was honest and open to talking about your past, present, and future. She obviously was mistaken. Because he was the only man, she had been close to in a while, and she was very close to him, she let down her guard and started to fall for him. On the other hand, Jalon tried to sleep, but he tossed and turned all morning. He got up and watched television, while Caroline just lay in bed and cried. She tried writing, but nothing came to mind. She tried reading, but she was not able to concentrate. She was not tired but restless and did not know what to do. Caroline was deeply saddened and depressed. She prayed to remove the negative emotions, but after a while, they only returned. In her mind, she knew she needed help, and something had to be done to resolve this deep feeling of hopelessness and depression. So, she called a friend who was a physician specializing in counseling and depression.

She called and scheduled an appointment for the next evening. While Jalon was up tired but went to work, he tried calling again and once again left a message, but to no avail. She did not return his calls. In the evening after work, he drove by her house, but her car was not in the driveway. He knocked on the door, and no one answered, so he went on his way home, saddened and worried about Caroline. That evening, Caroline was able to speak with the doctor. Though she was apprehensive, she talked and was able to get things out of her heart and mind. The doctor told her not to be afraid or embarrassed because it was her first time seeing a doctor about her depression and past issues. He told her it was healthy to speak to a doctor or counselor about her feelings. He asked about her past, and she went into detail with tears in her eyes. She was very emotional. She spoke a bit about the present circumstances that triggered her current feelings. After a two-hour session, they ended the session and scheduled another meeting for the following week. After this first session, Caroline expressed her gratitude for being able to speak with a professional who could help her. She stated she felt much better after their conversation. The session ended as they shook hands goodbye, and she left and went out shopping to pick up a few items needed at home. She was now more positive in her emotional state. She picked up her messages but was not in the mood to talk with Jalon. To prevent more hurt, she avoided and isolated herself from going to church and from him because she did not want to see him and ignite the emotional feelings she had for him. She continued her counseling and church hopping for a while. Jalon continued to call to see how she was doing, but she continued to ignore his calls.

Eventually, she reluctantly answered his call one day, but the conversation was short and to the point. She refused any offers to go out with him but retained their friendship from a distance. He was hurt, and so was Caroline. She eventually contacted her son and daughter-in-law and put them in charge of running the business for a while because she had a plan in mind, but it was not finalized yet. She continued to church hop, but she was very unhappy and lonely.

She was not able to do the things that were meaningful to her and to others anymore. So, Caroline finally made up her mind and planned to leave the country for Africa to do some missionary work.

"Love begins with a smile, grows with
a kiss, and ends with a teardrop"
Anonymous.

CHAPTER 6
VACATION TO AFRICA

She felt that since her business was doing well and her son was now in charge, she could leave. She spoke with her son and told him her plans. Since she had no husband or young children to attend to, she was free to go and do whatever she wanted to do. She felt a vacation, a trip would help her relieve her heart and mind, and she always wanted to go and help the less fortunate would be of great help, so she packed her bags, kissed her son and daughter-in-law goodbye, and left for Africa. Her goals were to help orphans, widows to teach and empower young women on how to run their own businesses, just as she did at home in the United States at the church. She took the vacation with a local airline that travels to countries she wanted to get acclimated to others that had already taken this journey to know more about the areas, the people and the needs. She met several new friends on her journey. Some women were in the same situation and predicament as hers, and others were widows and widowers finding ways and opportunities to use their talents to help others, while the rest were helping because they loved the Lord and enjoyed helping and serving others.

Caroline enjoyed what she was doing. In her spare time, she would continue to write, draw, and paint. Periodically, she would call her son and daughter-in-law to let them know she was doing well, and she would ask about Jalon because she never told him she was leaving. Periodically, when she called, her son would tell her that Jalon was asking about her and that he was praying for her, but most of the time, her reply would be, "Tell him I said hello." Jalon was distraught when he heard she left on a trip to Africa. It already hurt him when she left the church, but Africa! He was very surprised when he heard that, and there were not enough words to describe the pain he felt. But Caroline enjoyed the work she was doing, and everything was going well. She felt her life was now more meaningful being there, although she certainly missed her son and daughter-in-law. Shortly after, she received some good news: she would be a grandmother soon. She was very happy to hear that from her son the last time they spoke. She was still angry at Jalon but was more hurt by him not being truthful to her about the situation. Sometimes, at night when she went to bed, she still thought of him, but she knew deep in her heart she must release it and him to be free.

She knew the Scriptures very well about holding unforgiveness. She knew it was like eating poison and that eventually, it would kill her. After thinking about him that night and praying to the Lord, three months later, she called Jalon and spoke with him. He was very happy to hear her voice; he himself was speechless. She mostly did the talking, but he figured with time she would come around. However, she did not say much, just about the work she was doing, and he did not either because he did not know what to say except that he was sorry. Then shortly after, they got disconnected for some reason, and she was unable to reconnect with him because a hurricane warning was in effect for the coastal area where she was.

The next day, on the news, they saw severely damaged areas due to a hurricane that had passed through that region, and everyone was now worried about her safety. All the telephone circuits were down, or the lines were busy. Jalon now realized that the disconnection was because of the storm. He was very worried and afraid for her. All they could do at this time was pray for the safety of the people and Caroline.

Now Jalon and Caroline's son stayed in close contact because he and his wife continued to attend the church. About two weeks later, Caroline was able to call her son due to the severely damaged region. The destruction was devastating, and the cleanup was slow. Her son and daughter-in-law were very worried and were very happy to hear her voice. He cried because he didn't know what was going on or if she had made it through. "I am safe," she replied, "but we had three casualties in the camp I served in, and the surrounding areas had an enormous amount of destruction and death." She said food and water were scarce, but the group she was with had enough. She praised the Lord for sparing their lives and believed it was also because of the good deeds they were doing that the Lord saved them. She was not able to speak with Jalon because he was at work when she called.

After the conversation with her son, he called Jalon later that evening and let him know she was okay. It was a cry of relief for him. "Thank you, Lord," he cried as they ended the conversation. It had been almost a year since Caroline had been in Africa, and a few weeks after the storm, Caroline became very ill and ended up in the local hospital. They could not find what was wrong with her because they had very few doctors, the medical facility was not equipped, and they did not have the medication to treat her. The hospital was still severely damaged from the hurricane.

A chaplain from a local mission when she arrived became friends and called her son and told him she was very ill and in the hospital. He stated he was worried because she was running very high fevers. He said he had tried to call her several times, but there was no answer, and his mom could not talk to him. He assumed that was why he had not been receiving any return calls from her. The chaplain explained she didn't look good, she was not doing well, and they couldn't seem to find what was wrong with her. The chaplain put her on the phone to talk with her son, but her voice was so weak he could barely hear her. He wanted her to rest as much as she could to keep her strength up. He was very worried about his mom at this time. "I love you, Mom," he replied. "Hold on, be strong." The chaplain went back on the phone with her son and said, "It is best to send her home so she can get adequate care and so they can find out what is wrong with her." "I agree," he stated. "Call her doctor so they can contact the hospital there that she will be coming home." "Okay," he replied. The chaplain said, "I will put her on the mission plane as soon as possible," and her son said, "Thank you for calling. We will talk again soon." "Yes, sir! Goodbye," and he hung up the phone. Once again, he called on the church family, especially Jalon, to pray. As they prepared Caroline, they rushed her onto the plane that was on standby. The next day, they arrived at the airport in the U.S. Her son and daughter-in-law were waiting, and the ambulance was on standby to pick her up. As soon as the plane landed, they rushed her into the ambulance. Her son and daughter-in-law were at her side and had just a moment to say hello and kiss and hug his mom. He was tearful and emotional. His wife consoled him and encouraged him that everything would be all right. He wanted to be by his mom's side, but because of precautionary measures and not knowing what sickness she had, they told him it would be best and safest to follow the ambulance. Because she was worse off than he expected, she was going in and out of consciousness. As they arrived at the hospital, he called Jalon at the church because it was Bible study night. He explained the situation and asked once again for the congregation to pray for his mother.

"One of the greatest love a person can give is to save a life"

1 John 3:16

CHAPTER 7

LIFE THREATENING SITUATION

Jalon was happy Caroline had returned, but he was not happy to hear about her condition; he was hurt once again to hear that she was very ill. The ambulance arrived at the hospital emergency room entrance, and her son was once again at her side, holding her hand, telling her to hold on and that he loved her. He urged her to hold on because her grandbaby was soon to arrive. They placed her in isolation while she was in the emergency room and started blood work, x-rays, and other necessary tests immediately. Her son and daughter-in- law had to answer many questions outside of her room and signed consent forms while the medical staff continued working and preparing her for whatever was necessary to save her life. He stayed by her side as she was still in and out of consciousness. Eventually, they moved her quickly to the intensive care unit of the hospital in private isolation because they were not sure what was going on with her. Since she had been out of the country for a while on a mission trip, they had to intubate her because she took a turn for the worse and became unconscious. They were waiting for the blood work results to determine what was wrong with her.

Jalon called to find out how she was doing. Her son started to cry, and Jalon asked what was wrong. His heart throbbed because he knew it was serious, and pain gripped his heart. He stated, "My mom went into a coma." "My God," Jalon exclaimed! The son explained that they were still working on her and waiting for the blood work results. Jalon tried to control himself and consoled her son the best way he knew how. "Let us pray," he said. They prayed for a short while, and then Jalon mentioned that he would call on the whole church family once again to pray. He added that as soon as he finalized things, he would come down as soon as possible. "Just remember she is a strong woman, a fighter. She has been through something before and made it through. She will go through this again. God has Caroline in His hands. She has work to do," he stated. "God is not ready for her yet!" These words seemed to comfort the young man's heart. Before they hung up the phone, Jalon prayed for comfort and strength.

He then called some more kinfolk and let them know the situation with Caroline and that she was back home. Finally, the results of the blood work arrived, along with the x-rays and MRI. The doctors quickly discussed the results and the necessary treatment. The results revealed that Caroline had a major infectious disease that affected her kidneys, causing life-threatening kidney failure and shock. They had to move quickly to save her life. They brought in the hemodialysis team to start treatment and antibiotics while the doctors talked with Caroline's son and family. They had arrived at the hospital and were concluding on the next steps. After the treatment, there was no change, and they had to make a final decision quickly because Caroline's kidneys were failing fast.

The doctor arrived and spoke with the family again, saying, "The bad news is she will need a kidney transplant." They were in awe! They did not think it was that serious, but it was. They held each other and started to cry. The doctor said they needed to move fast to find a kidney donor. They talked it over as the doctors stepped away to let them discuss among themselves. Shortly after, they spoke with the doctors and said they would do whatever they could to save her life. The doctors mentioned that they would draw blood from potential donors for tissue typing. They started drawing blood from the family to see if there was a possible match. The physicians also said they would check the kidney donors' list for any possible matches. "Thank you," her son replied. "We will call as many friends and family as we can to see if they would be willing to come to get checked out to see if there is a possible match." "Great idea," the doctor said. The family gathered around Caroline's bed and prayed for her, the situation, and the strength of their families. They encouraged her and each other to stay strong and reminded her that they loved her very much.

Once again, Caroline's son had to call on Jalon and let him know what was happening, asking the church family for prayers and those willing and able to come to get checked to see if they were a possible match. Jalon's heart was grieved and heavy from the bad news because the woman he loved was in a coma and could possibly die. He shed a tear while he prayed. It was hard for him to think about this, as he had not seen her in almost a year since they last spoke in person. But he said okay to her son and called on all the church family immediately. One by one, Caroline's family started their workup to see if there was a possible match to be a donor. The church family also arrived and began their workup. After a while, Caroline's family and the church family joined hands together in prayers for her life. The word spread fast, and many people showed up that evening and the next day to be tested. Jalon tried to stop by the hospital room to see Caroline, but he was too distraught. His heart could not bear to see her in that condition, lying there, unable to do anything about her condition but pray and cry. Her son and daughter-in-law stayed by her side all night, along with a few family members. The next day, she was a bit stronger but still in and out of consciousness. Her daughter-in-law finally went home and brought food and a change of clothing for her husband because he would not leave his mother's side.

Around noon the next day, the doctors came with good news. They explained that it must have been a miracle because this does not happen very often. They stated they had been doctors for many years, and most people waiting for a kidney donor, or a transplant usually die, or it takes a while before there is a donor. But in this case, they had found a donor and a perfect match for Caroline. "Thank God!" her son yelled. "Who is it?" he asked. "We thought you knew," the doctor explained. "It was one of your family members. Now time is of the essence. We must move quickly. We will explain the procedure as we prepare them both." They needed to get Caroline ready immediately. "Also, we must go now. Continue to pray for us too. We will talk later and keep you updated." As they prepared both patients and pushed them into the operating room, the procedure began shortly after. It would take several hours under the skillful hands of the surgeons. The family began to pray, talking with the Lord and thanking Him for the donor, for Caroline, and for the skillful hands of the doctors. They prayed for protection during the operation. They were astonished to see that the Lord had sent a donor so quickly, a first in the history of their careers. They were happy for Caroline, acknowledging that she deserved it after caring for the less fortunate in Africa. A few hours later, the surgeries were successful, and they were finally over.

As the family waited anxiously to hear the news, one of the doctors from the operating room approached them. They waited with anticipation. He smiled as he approached, and they clapped their hands and praised God. "The surgery was a success," he stated. "There were no complications, but we must monitor her closely. We did the best we knew how. They will be out shortly and placed in the progressive care unit or the recovery room for close monitoring. It will depend on Caroline's sustainability and progress." "Thank you, and God's blessings be upon you all," the doctors replied. They went on their way. About an hour later, they wheeled Caroline out to the progressive care unit. She was doing well, her skin color was returning to normal, and her vital signs were stable. But she was still under the influence of anesthesia and not fully responsive. She was not entirely out of danger yet, but the nurse in charge of her care in the recovery room was carefully monitoring her progress.

As the family sat by her bedside and continued to pray for both patients, her son asked the nurse when they could see any significant progress or change and when they would know she was out of danger. The nurse stated that the first 24 to 72 hours were the most critical times. Then they asked about the donor. The nurse explained that there had been a small complication, and they were still attending to the patient. "That is all the information I can give you at this time," she said. "Oh no!" they exclaimed. "We are so sorry. We did not know. We hope everything will be okay. We will continue to pray, they added, realizing that their focus had been mainly on Caroline and not the donor. They were very worried and continued to pray for the donor. They still did not know which family member had donated their kidney. As things were moving fast, they prayed earnestly for both patients' speedy recovery.

The next day, they saw positive changes occurring with Caroline. Her skin color was back to normal, and she was responding to stimuli. They inquired about the donor who had given the kidney. The nurse stated the complication was resolved, but the patient could not have any visitors at this time due to immunity and infection concerns. She added that once the doctor gave the okay, the family could visit. The patient was very exhausted from the second surgery and complications, so they needed their rest. "Just continue to pray. I believe all will be well." It was now late in the evening, and no one had eaten, so they went to the cafeteria to have dinner. It was a great sigh of relief because a kidney had been found, and Caroline's life was prayerfully out of danger. After a short while, some of them went home. Caroline's daughter-in- law went home to shower and rest, as she was now in her eighth month of pregnancy and getting bigger each day.

Early the next morning, she brought her husband a change of clothes and some breakfast. The following day, Caroline was breathing on her own, and things seemed to be improving. On the third day, she woke up fully conscious but could hardly speak due to the intubation tubes in her throat. She looked around the room, unaware that she was back home in the US or that she was in the hospital. She only knew that all her family was with her and felt a bit disoriented but stable. They all praised God for the miracle recovery and the kidney she received. The doctors quickly rushed in to check her out when they heard she was awake. They wanted to ensure everything was okay. "The kidney seems to be functioning as it should," one of the doctors stated to the family. They tried to explain the situation and her condition that led to her being in the hospital, but she was still very tired from all the medications and dozed off to sleep again.

The rest of the family left, and more visitors came by with cards, balloons, and well-wishes. While she was dozing off, Caroline's son called Jalon to give him an update on her condition and share the good news. The phone rang several times and went to voicemail. He left a message saying, "Mom is doing much better. She is now awake, alert, and stable, and her new kidney seems to be functioning normally. Thank you for your prayers and help! Hope to see you soon. Bye for now. We will talk again soon." He hung up the phone. He inquired once again about the donor, but while they were focusing on Caroline's recovery, the donor had been discharged home. "We need to know which family member donated their kidney for mom," her son asked. "I'm sorry," the nurse said. "The donor left a note stating they do not want any attention and just want everyone to be thankful that God used the donor as a blessing."

Jalon returned the call to Caroline's son, but it went to voicemail. "I am so happy to hear the good news. Praise God, all is well!" he stated. "See you soon. I hope you understand why I did not stop by. It is a very sensitive situation and circumstances concerning our relationship. I did not want to be there and upset her while she was in a coma. They can hear your voice while they are under, and I did not want my voice to cause any alarm that could have worsened her condition. Bye for now."

'Love is the beauty of the soul"
Saint Augustine

CHAPTER 8

STAGE OF HEALING

When she was fully awakened the next day, Caroline's son and daughter-in-law was at her bedside, she was excited to see them she hugged and kissed her son and he hugged and kissed her and grabbed her by the neck and cried tears of joy, Caroline said to her daughter-in-law come closer because she was now at eight months in her pregnancy, she rubbed her stomach and they both cried as she bent down to hug her mother in law, your grandbaby will be here soon she replied so get well soon. They explained the circumstances and situation that caused her to be in the hospital they explained to her the surgery she underwent due to the illness she contracted while she was in Africa on the missionary trip. It all seems like a blur to her because she was sick for a while and was in and out of consciousness from there to here. The next few days, she was feeling much stronger and was able to get out of bed and exercise, taking short walks with assistance. The next day she asked the nurse to take her to the room where the donor was located so she could say thanks, the nurse told her the donor was discharged and went home! Oh, she said why so quickly she asked, I will find out that answer and let you know the nurse responded. Because she knew to herself as a nurse the discharge was certainly too fast, so she went to and check into why the patient was discharged that early. A few hours later the nurse returned and spoke with Caroline and said there was a mixed up with the charts of the patients that was in the room one patient was discharged and the other was transferred to another floor! And did not want any recognition or any praise in donating the kidney. "Wow" Caroline replied that is certainly a modest person. Yes! The nurse replied.

Caroline then said to the nurse, seeing the condition that I was in and almost lost my life, I am sure you would understand, could you please bend the rules for my sake! What is that the nurse asked Caroline? I heard it's a family member that donated the kidney to me and I am begging you please, even though they do not want to be recognized, I beg of you could you please as she whispered give me the room number and I will find my way there on my own, no one will have to know. I know nothing, the nurse replied! As she scribbled a room number on a small piece of paper from her pocket and "accidentally" dropped it on the floor as she walked away and said I will see you later Caroline, get some rest. Caroline smiled and said I will! Thank you! As she slowly arose from her bed and picked up a small, folded piece of paper. Everyone was gone for the day including her son and her daughter-in-law. She opened a small piece of paper and quickly peaked at the number as she smiled, thinking of how she would sneak out and get up to the room.

Caroline requested a wheelchair, to get around. She slowly pushed herself in the wheelchair towards the elevator and located the floor on that little piece of paper the nurse gave her but when she went to the floor into the room the bed was empty and made up, they had taken the patient to therapy due to complications. Caroline was happy but at the same time sad because she wanted very much to give her gratitude to whomever donated the kidney to save her life. So, while she waited for a while she praised the Lord for scaring her life. This was the first time she had a little time to herself without the visitors interrupting her speaking with the Lord and giving him thanks. She talked to the Lord about the trip to Africa for a short while and waited a while longer and eventually returned to her room to rest because she was getting tired. She said to herself "I'll get some rest, and we'll return later by that time I believe they will be back." When she arrived at her room there was a few family members waiting there to see her she was surprised because of the visit from an old friend, by the name of "Pam" a physical therapist that helped her during her visits at the clinic while she was recovering from the accident when she broke her arm. They become close friends during that period of time. She had stopped by after hearing from a friend what had happened to Caroline, because they had lost contact during her visit to Africa, now she was happy to see her but not under the circumstances once again. They had a lot to talk about and a lot to catch up on.

The family members stayed and spoke with her for a short while then hugged and prayed with her. They were happy to see the speedy recovery and what the Lord had done. A short while after they went home. Pam greeted her once again with a big, long hug and kiss, as Caroline talked about her mission trip and the work she was doing when she was there in Africa, and how much she enjoyed helping the people and felt she accomplished something meaningful while she was there, then I became sick and ended up back in the US, in the hospital. Caroline said "praise God I am still alive; the Lord sees fit to keep me going" Amen! To that says Pam. Caroline told him she was still a bit this quieted the nurse. Because of a friend she was getting close to, a male friend she replied he was not completely honest and truthful about some things and that hurts me deeply." Pam said, it sounds as if you were getting close to this person! Actually, it sounds to me as if you were interested and could have been falling in love.

Yes! Caroline says, I was very much interested, and I was heartbroken when I heard some things and I had to ask him about it, it sounds as if you are still bothered by it says Pam! Yes! Caroline replied. Pam says, as long as you are not holding unforgiveness! Is there! No Caroline replied, I do not, but it is certainly hard not to think about it without getting upset. I guess because of my" past" let it go replied to Pam, so things will not eat away at you like cancer. You are right Caroline says, I will ask the Lord more earnestly to help me with this. Thank you for listening and stopping by to visit me. You're welcome, Pam replied then she asked when are you going home? When you are discharged from the hospital what are your plans once you get well, are you planning to go back to Africa on the mission again? Caroline replied, "I think I will take a break for a while and be led by the Lord and see how things go.

Pam asks, I would like to invite you to visit the church I am presently attending, the word is a rich and the pastor is very anointed he bring strong and powerful messages each time he teaches, that is when you are feeling better off course! And if you do not mind visiting other churches, "no not at all I would love to reply to Caroline"! At this time, I was still searching, when I left for Africa. "Okay that's great sounds like a plan," Pam replied. It's getting late, and you need your rest I am so happy to see you and glad that things worked out well for you and you're doing much better God bless and have a good evening and we will talk and see each other again soon, bye for now as they embraced and hug each other, and don't forget to call me when you discharge from the hospital! Let me know as soon as you get home, so I can stop by or just in case you need anything. Okay Pam Caroline, thanks again, and as she walked out of the room, she waved goodbye! And gestured lack of hugs and kisses, I love you. Shortly after the nurse came in and gave her the last doses of her evening medications and then she went to bed.

The next morning Caroline daughter in law and son stop by to see how she was doing, Nock! Nock! But Caroline with deep in sleep and she did not hear the door waited was opened so they quietly approached and sat down till she was fully awaked, good morning mom says her son how are you feeling today? In a gentle tone because he did not want to startle her because she was still asleep and was not expecting anyone to be in her room, good morning, Caroline replied, I am doing much better, I feel much stronger than I was, last, I remember when I was in Africa. To the operating room and Thank God! Good morning said her daughter-in-law! Again, Caroline replied to good morning! They approached the bed and embraced her with a kiss on the cheek and a hug. I was so worried about you personally stated I thought I was going to lose you this time! You have been through a lot of moms, but God's hands are on your life truly God's hand is on your life! And you are still here thanked God for family, we are still trying to find out the family member that donated their kidney to you. We visited and they said there were some complications, and they had to go back to the operating room and since then we have not heard anything else, I hope all is well! Then Caroline said, I tried to visit earlier but there was no one in the room. The nurse told me the person was discharged home and there was some misunderstanding and did not want to be identified. Wow! Caroline's son stated to be such a modest person and now I am certainly curious to find out which one of the family members it is. Shortly after there was a knock on the door, come in Caroline stated! At the visitor entered the door they were all in anticipation to see who it was, to her surprise it was Jalon, with a beautiful vase full of red roses and a get-well card and balloons, good morning he stated to everyone with a smile on his face! Son, he said to Caroline son I have received all your messages and thank you for keeping me up to date I would like to apologize that I am just able to get away and return to visit, school and attending to church businesses and I was also on my knees praying for Caroline, we understand her excuse themselves stated and shook his hand and greet his wife, he approached Caroline with a warm smile! And greeted her. with a kiss on her cheek, and a warm gentle embrace. These are for you! They are beautiful, she stated thank you! As she took them from his hands and she smelled the flowers and then placed them on the nightstand table, I will read the card later if you don't mind, no not at all he stated, and she tied the balloon on the side of the bed rail. You are welcome, he replied, and how are you feeling? He asked, she replied I am feeling much better than before it is so good to see you thanks for stopping by you are welcome it my pleasure, I wish I could have arrived sooner! Then she replied how are you doing Jalon? He says I am doing okay now! Now that I know you are okay. That is great! She replied with a smile on her face because they put them in her heart, she was excited and happy to see him, the anger she felt towards him had dissipated, and joy filled her heart when she saw him again. And he was happy to see her too. He stayed for a short while and stated he would return to see her soon, he had some urgent business to finalize, he was very happy to see that she was doing well then said goodbye with an embrace and kiss. And shook her son's hand then he left. It was not long after there was another knock on the door, it was the nurse stopping by doing her morning rounds of medication treatment and care. Her son and daughter-in-law excused themselves while the nurse was doing treatment and care for Caroline. Good morning, how are you today? The nurse stated! I am doing great, replied to Caroline. The nurse replied that is wonderful, I am happy to see you are doing much better today and you do look better I would say! Thank you, she replied as the nurse continued to her morning treatment. While the nurse was caring for her, she thought about Jalon's visit. The nurse completed their treatment and told her she would see her later, as she exited the door her son and daughter-in-law entered.

I am so glad I am alive to be here to welcome my soon coming grandbaby! Caroline stated, yes mom! That is right her son yelled we are happy too, we are so glad you are feeling much better, me too, said Caroline. We will not be staying too much longer, we just wanted to see if you needed anything because we are still a bit tired, okay I understand, said Caroline go home and get some rest! I am certainly doing much better now! Thank you both for the support and love, I will call you when I see the doctor again and when I am released to go home. Okay, said her daughter-in-law, we love you! Kisses and hugs, bye we will talk with you later.

Caroline was very curious and wanted to go by once again to see the donor that evening, but she was over exhausted, after her exercises and therapy throughout the day she went in afterwards and fell asleep and woke up the next morning. She was now out of the progressive care unit and went on a regular floor specifically for renal patients. During the morning hours Caroline's intentions was to stop by the donors will once again, she was strong enough to dress herself and get out of bed into a wheelchair that was at the side of her bed and transport herself to the room since it was now on the same floor a little way at the opposite end of the building down the hall, it would have been too far to walk, she entered the room but the patients in the bed said it was the wrong room, it might be next door he stated, so she really herself next door, before she entered the room she knocked on the door but there was no answer, she peeked in but she noticed the curtains was drawn for "privacy "so she hesitated to disturb the person but deep down in her heart she wanted to see who it was and to say thank you! As she pulled closer to the curtains and said hello, my name is Caroline, I am so sorry to disturb your rest, but I am searching for someone that did a wonderful thing for me and I was wondering if it was you! That is a wonderful thing is a kidney, someone donated one of their kidneys to save my life as she continued to talk tears fell and she started to cry. The person was also sitting in a wheelchair looking through the window, then a gentle but familiar voice answered her and said come in, but what she heard as familiar and thought in her mind could not be possible as she thinks about it and was wondering if she was hearing the right thing. As she slowly pulled curtains to the side, the person's back was facing her direction watching television and was also peeking through the window. The person was covered up with a white robe and a blanket trying to stay warm. As she tried to compose herself by drying the tears on her face, she gently said once again, I am sorry to disturb you but I'm Caroline and I need to know, and wanted to meet with you and to thank you, I heard you are the one that saved my life and I am grateful, and also her you are next to Kin, I do know I have some of our relatives out of state and out of the country that I have never met before and my son told me they called everyone from everywhere that would be willing to donate a kidney. While Caroline talked the person sat quietly and listened, then she asked what is your name?

Then the person slowly turned around facing Caroline, and when she saw the face, she was in disbelief, she did not know what to say, she was now lost for words, she started to cry! She tried to compose herself as she rolled her wheelchair closer to the bedside and embraced him, then she said what are you doing here? Then he said, "I am he; I am the one who donated the kidney to save your life. I have no regrets and if I could have helped, I would not have done it any other way. I also know if it were me, you would have done the same for me! Caroline was still in awe! And she cried even more when she heard those words coming out of Jalon's mouth. She asked Why? Why did you do this for me! He stated because I care, and I would rather lose a kidney than to see you die. They both cried and embraced each other, Jalon, said I am truly happy to see you back, but I wish it was under better circumstances. Caroline replied the same.

It has been a year since you went away, I was so worried about you, but all I could do was to pray, but here you are the Lord has brought you back. So how are you feeling now! She said much better than the Lord how about you she replied, he said great! As he pulled back part of his down and showed her the scar where they removed the kidney. As Caroline once again started to cry tears of joy, no more tears Jalon replied. Thank God you are here, I heard how bed you were when you got here in the hospital, I did not have the heart to go up and see you like that, but here you are now. I remembered that the last time we spoke it was a wild back, I did not hear the complete conversation because of the static on the phone lines prior to the hurricane and shortly after the was disconnected.

What were you doing in Africa, he asked? I was on a mission trip helping the widows and orphans and I was teaching and empowering the woman to start their own businesses. I truly enjoyed that, it was very meaningful to me and during my spare time I continued to write, paint and draw, which is great, he replied, "How about you Caroline asked? Well, I am still helping out at the church, and have completed school. That is great news congratulations she says. I must leave you now so you can get some rest, I am getting a bit tired again, I myself am getting back into bed, do you know when you are going home? She asked! I am not sure, I will find out and let you know, okay she says.

Jalon asked, "would you mind giving me the phone number to your room so we could talk, further sometime, absolutely she replied. And gave him the phone number, she embraced him and pushed her wheelchair towards the door and went to her room. She had no visitors that day, just a few phone calls to see how she was doing. Although she was tired, she laid down and was not able to go to sleep, because of the surprise of what just took place and finding out that Jalon was the donor and extended such a gift to her, he sacrificed something that was very valuable to save her life.

Jalon did not talk about it because he was not the kind of man to brag or boast about anything he does; he was just a humble soul! If it were up to him, it would be kept anonymous, but Caroline was so grateful she had to share the good news with all who she knew, a few hours later heard Dr. stop by and told her she was doing very well, and her kidneys were functioning at optimal level. And he was getting ready to release her and discharge her for home soon.

The next morning there was a knock on the door, come in she replied it was Jalon he was dressed and ready to go home, good morning he stated, how are you feeling today? Caroline replied I am doing well, and you she asked? He replied splendidly, as he approached her and embraced her with a kiss on her cheeks as he usually does. As you can see, I am going home. My doctors stopped by yesterday and said I am doing very well so there was no need for me to stay here any longer. I was happy to hear that good news; is there anything I can do for you before I leave? Caroline replied no! Thank you for asking. I truly appreciate your kindness; you have done more than enough. Well then, I will be leaving now, will you stay in touch, he asked! Sure, Caroline replied. Take good care of yourself, as he approached her Caroline stretched out her arms as a gesture, to hug him before you leave so he embraced her with a hug and kissed her once again on her cheeks, bye for now! As he heads towards the door. She was still amazed by him and was no longer feeling anger towards him, as she thought about it a few tears fell. She remembered the get-well card he gave her that she forgot to read, and quickly opened the envelope and read it. It stated, my dearest Caroline, I pray nothing but the best for you and hope you recover speedily with the help and grace of God! And may God continue blessings be upon your life, with all my love Jalon. She cried as she read those beautiful words that he expressed were heartfelt and she knew he meant every word of it; she wiped away the tears from her eyes as she reminisced on the past and present. She spent another week in the hospital and many other visitors and family she had not seen for years showed up, and some she does not even know or remember, it was a sad but pleasant reunion because of the circumstances. Then finally she was discharged to go home, she had to have regular follow up visits with her primary care physician and a renal specialist for follow up care, she had a lot of offers to help out at home when she gets there. The doctor told her she needed to watch her diet and watch what she eats very careful an hour later her daughter-in-law picked her up from the hospital waiting room and dropped her home, her friend Pam was waiting at the house to help with anything she needed.

"Nothing can bring you peace but yourself".
Ralf W. Emerson

CHAPTER 9

HOME SWEET HOME

WELCOME HOME! Pam yelled and was standing outside by the door waiting to assist and help her out of the car, they embraced each other with big hugs and kisses. "I am so happy you are finally home she stated, I am happy to be home said Caroline I can now relax in my own home in my own bed.

Her daughter-in-law was very happy she was out of the hospital and was finally home too, she gave her a big hug and kissed her goodbye and as she drove away, she waved and Caroline yelled, we will talk later tell my son I love him and I love you too as they each waved good-bye. Now, said Pam you need to get some rest and leave all else to me, okay Caroline replied, Pam said I already prepared something for you to eat while you rest Oh thank you that so kind of you said Caroline. Since I have made you have been a good friend, I appreciate you taking the time out to help me Caroline said to Pam, then Pam replied and said I am sure you would have done the same for me if I was in this situation absolutely, she replied. This was the second time in a week she had heard that phrase, so said Caroline "we caught up with me in the hospital, I apologize I am so sorry I did not ask how are you doing? And how are things with you!

Pam stated not much, just work as usual! That is all. Caroline replied you are too beautiful, and gorgeous woman not to do more with your life, you are right said Pam! I just have not found the time yet to sit down and evaluate what else I wanted to do and get involved with, what about the relationship Caroline ask to know she replied not yet I am waiting until the Lord send the right one my way. Amen to that, said Caroline. As they continued to talk Pam asked the question are you hungry? No replied Caroline I had eaten at the hospital before I was discharged, okay get some rest and I will put away what I made for later okay that sounds great.

A few hours later, Caroline woke up and had a sandwich and some fruit cup of juice that Pam had prepared for her, she still was not very hungry because she was excited to be home, Caroline stated that Pam the friend I spoke about at the hospital? Yes, I recall, the one you seemed to be upset with, yes! Replied Caroline. I saw him in the hospital, what was wrong with him, Pam asked? Nothing I went to visit the donors, and he was the one that donated his kidney to me that is great Pam said WOW! That is truly a blessing in disguise! Pam was very surprised and was in awe, then she asked Caroline how you feel, Caroline stated she was in shock herself and was no longer angry or bitter with him, WOW! Pam stated a man that have given up a kidney has to be in love with you, no one will just give up his or her kidney for you. As those words left her lips Caroline started to break down and cry once again as she thought about her life could have been lost if there were not no one to donate a kidney to her, Pam consoled her friend and reminded her that everything is going to be okay. As they talked and caught up, the evening went by fast, Caroline was very happy with the companionship and was also happy to see her friend that evening they had ordered in and watch television.

and shortly after Caroline called her son and daughter-in-law chat for a while and shortly after went to bed.

The next day, they slept in late, and they had a nice breakfast and talked, afterword's Caroline called Jalon that afternoon and let him know that she was doing well, and she had arrived home. He was very excited to hear her voice, and she was too. He was very happy to hear the good news, he asked her if she needed anything she stated she was fine and had everything she needed, because her friend Pam was with her. She asked him how he was feeling, and if everything was well, he said he was doing well! She thanked him for the flowers, balloons and card "I wanted to thank you once again especially for that card with those beautiful words you had given to me, I am sorry I did not get to call you as much while I was there, I understand he replied, I know you needed to rest and have other visitors, Yes! She stated, and thanks for all you have done by saving my life, they talked for a while and before they hung up, he prayed with her, we will talk again soon, yes! We will she replied to buy! Pam smiled but did not say a word. After the conversation Pam reminded Caroline that as soon as she felt much better, she would pick her up for church services and she nodded her head yes! Pam stayed two more days and then went home, because she took a few days off from work to help Caroline and had to return to work the next day. She called and thanked her for the help and the time together.

Caroline followed up with her regular doctor's appointment as scheduled, the doctors said she was recovering well, and the wounds were healing well. She traveled by facility transportation, because she did not feel comfortable to drive and her son stop by later that evening to check on her, they were happy to see each other and talked for a while and was very happy she was doing well, he did not stay very long but brought food just in case she needed something to eat later that evening.

The next day, Caroline stopped by the store and brought a thank you card for the church family to thank them for their prayers, love and support, she mailed it and during the Sunday service they read it to the congregation. The next few weeks she had many visitors stop by to check on her and offered to help! It was about six weeks later Pam called and told her it was time to get out "I will be picking you up on Sunday for service, you promise to come with me to visit I hope you are up to it." Caroline said, she was ready to get out because she was getting bored and needed to get out and she was feeling much better." I feel like a new woman Caroline stated" okay Pam replied, that is great! I will see you on Sunday at 10 AM sharp! Services start at 11 AM, Pam replied. By for now Pam replied see you on Sunday and Caroline said the same and Hong up.

Caroline was focused on some work she needed to get done for the next two days on the Internet for her business, she stayed up late that evening and she did a small amount of writing and reading as well, she reminisced on the past few weeks what had happened to her and that goodness of the Lord that speared her life.

Early the next morning was Sunday she was a bit slower than usual, but she got up and showered, got dressed styled their hair and put her makeup on, she was excited to go to church and here a fresh word. She quickly made a cup of coffee and toast to hold her over until she left the service. It was not long after Pam arrived, and the doorbell was ringing! Caroline grabbed her purse and hurried to the door, well good morning she said to Pam and hug her good morning to you too, how are you today! I am doing wonderful Caroline replied and yourself! Caroline asked Pam to reply on doing well also, that is wonderful as they smiled and hugged each other. Thank you for picking me up Caroline replied Pam said you're welcome and thank you for coming and keeping your promise, you are certainly a woman of your word. As they headed towards the car, they complemented each other on how beautiful they looked. Then Caroline asks, "is this a new church? Pam answered yes! Fairly new it was opened about eight months ago, but it is growing because we have an awesome pastor. It is about 25 minutes' drive from here, but it was very comforting to know where she was going the world, and the message was rich. They finally arrived at the church and were greeted by friendly and pleasant ushers who deseeded them at the third row from the pulpit.

The worship and praise team were singing and clapping their hands worshiping the Lord, as they sang, she felt the presence of the Holy Spirit moving in the sanctuary and her spirit was uplifted as she clapped her hands and song she thought once again on the goodness of the Lord and how far and where he has brought her. Shortly after the worship and praise service they prayed and introduced the speaker and pastor, as he arrived up to the pulpit Caroline was in astonishment, because she could not believe her eyes and ears, the pastor was no other than" Jalon" she was speechless, and she was now wondering if the Lord was trying to convey something to her. As he greeted the congregation and, well, all the new visitors he prayed that the Lord would use him and that the message would be a blessing to the people. His message and topic were on. "LOVE and FORGIVENESS."

As Caroline sat and looked on, she gently nudged Pam and said, "You will not believe what is going on, she asked what you mean! Then Caroline said, the pastor that is about to preach I know him, how do you know him Pam asks? Caroline replied and said, it is Jalon, the donor of my kidney, Pam was lost for words but was only able to say what a small world we would talk about later.

So as Jalon was about to start his sermon, Caroline tried to be inconspicuous and try to calm herself down, but she was now very much overwhelmed and started to cry as the word went forth, it was an awesome and powerful word. Pam cried too, because it touched her heart deeply as the ushers attended by passing out tissues. In about an hour and a half the service was over then they gave the benediction followed by altar call and for those who needed prayers to come at the altar then shortly after a few announcements and the service was over shortly after. Many people greeted each other and welcomed the new visitors while the pastor had it towards the door where he created and shook the hands of everyone before they left the service. But Caroline and Pam waited at the end of the line as they left. As they approached, Pam shook his hand and gave him accolades that it was a great message and a great word, then she said this is my friend and introduced Caroline to him he was surprised and lost for words because she did not see her he was very happy to see her and she was very happy to see him they shook hands and hugged her, he asked how she was feeling Caroline replied very well and said thank you also for that awesome message I was certainly blessed by it I needed that! Thank you he replied for coming! It was so good to see you both hope to see you again soon Jalon replied, thank you we will! Jalon wanted to talk a bit longer, but he had to uphold the professional standards as the pastor so he said, "we will talk later" "absolutely she replied", he wanted to hug her once again because he was so happy to see her once again it was a total surprise to him and her! As they said goodbye and walked away, he gazed at

Caroline as she walked away. This was the first time he saw her since she was discharged from the hospital, but they speak on a regular basis.

They headed out towards the car in the parking lot. As they drove away Caroline requested to stop at the restaurant so they could eat and talk. I enjoyed the service Caroline said to Pam, I thank you once again for inviting me, it was good that I came out. Was that a coincidence, she asked? Pam replied there are no coincidences, just divine appointments! Wow! Caroline stated, the Lord must be trying to show you something you need to pray and ask him what Pam said. Caroline replied, "You are right; I do believe that. They entered the restaurant and was seated by the waitress and was attended to immediately. They ate, chatted, and laughed, it was a wonderful afternoon we must do this again Caroline replied, I surely enjoyed myself today! Pam stated, now I am full and am about to go to sleep, let us go so you and I can go home and get some rest.

She dropped by her home and kissed her and said goodbye, we will talk later Caroline replied as she walked away towards her front doorsteps with the keys in her hands ready to open the door as her thoughts and mind reflected on the service and Jalon. Later that evening, Jalon called, and said truly I thank you for visiting today, I truly hope you were blessed, and I hope it is not too late to call. Caroline replied, no it's not too late to call and yes, I did enjoy the service, then Jalon said, by the way you looked beautiful today and I wanted to tell you that, but you know I had to uphold my professional standard, and I also wanted to ask another question, I hope it's not too much to ask, or out of context! What is it Caroline replied, what is your question! Then he said, "I would like to see you and speak with you in person, is there any day this week we can meet somewhere and grab a bite to eat and talk! Yes! she says with great anticipation in her voice, I will be free on Friday, how about 6pm? Ok Jalon replied, that is great, I will see you on Friday! Then Caroline said, "was this a coincident or what the way we met at the church," Jalon replied and said, there are no coincidences in God, just divine appointments! Now this is something else, what does Jalon ask? She said that "metaphor" this is the second time I have heard that this week, that's good Jalon replied. They talked for about 20 minutes, then said good night. She could hardly sleep, as she meditated on their conversation and anticipation of their meeting on Friday.

She wondered what he wanted to talk about! Jalon himself could hardly sleep that night as he reminisced on the service at church, seeing Caroline and talking with her, he was also anticipating their meeting on Friday. She continued with her routine work as usual at home because her business was mainly by internet, so it was easy to follow up with her scheduled doctor's appointments. Her son and daughter-in-law called after a while to see if she needed anything. After the conversation with her son, Caroline remembered that she did not thanked Jalon appropriately, so she thought of buying him a thank you card and was thinking of something meaningful and special to give him and now that they will be meeting on Friday, so she figured this would be a perfect opportunity to give him this memento. Caroline took a break and hurried to the gift shop, because she had the perfect gift in mind to buy for Jalon, she found what she was looking for and purchased it along with a thank you card. She had it carefully wrapped and decorated to her taste and placed into a beautiful gift bag. She was very excited, with a smile on her face she was eager with anticipation and made it home quickly since it was a few minutes away from her home.

The week went by fast and it was now Friday, as she waits in anticipation to meet with Jalon, three hours later, he arrived on time, he was in her drive way he honked the car horn once to let her know he was there, then he walked to the door and rand the door bell, she quickly picks up her purse, keys and gift bag and rushed towards the door, he was waiting patiently for her went she opened the door. Hello, he replied, Hello! Caroline says as he gently embraced her and as she locked the door behind her, hold her hand as she walked down the steps towards the car., as they approached, he quickly opens the car door for her until she sat down then closed the door afterword, she said thank you! As he entered the driver's seat, she asked how you are today! And he replied, great! it is a blessed and beautiful day, thank you for asking, how about yours! It is wonderful she stated, and you are also looking beautiful, thank you, she complimented him also and said you do not look bad yourself, and they both laughed as he drove off to their destination. Where are we going? She asked, a small acquainted Brazilian Restaurant the next town over he replied, "I love Brazilian cuisine" Caroline replied. Great! Jalon replied the food is tantalizing there I hope you enjoy it.

As soon as they arrived, they proceeded to seat them in a quite secluded spot for two, because he called in and made reservations ahead of time, a sort moment later the waitress attended to their needs and a handed them the menu's and proceeded by asking them what they wanted to drink and water proceeded to bring that order, then proceeded by telling them about the appetizers and the specials of the day and some of the great dishes to choose from. She stepped away and gave them a moment to decide what they wanted. They ordered appetizers followed by the main course. The appetizers arrived quickly as they sat and continued to talk, then Caroline remembered the gift she had brought along for Jalon, she said this is for you, I thought this you be the most appropriate time, as she hands over the small bag, wow! He said, you should not have! Yes, she replied, it is not much, you deserve more I just wanted to say thanks You!

As Jalon took the small bag and opened it, He wondered what it was and proceeded to pick up and open the card first and read it" You are one of the most kind and deserving person I have ever met, I just want to let you know I truly appreciate what you have done for me; may God Continual Blessings be upon your life… Love Always Caroline." The words she wrote touched him deeply, as he proceeded to say thank you, he then opened the beautifully wrapped Gift, as he opened it, he saw a beautiful crystal engraved memento with his name on it, it reads "TO: JALON A GREAT & WONDERFUL HERO AND ANGEL GOD SEND TO SAVE MY LIVE". He stared at it because it was beautiful and well thought out, and as the words penetrated his heart tears of joy flowed down his cheeks, he was lost for words a moment of silence and Caroline was emotional too, then he said "If I had to do it all over again I would do it for you! She started crying even more when she heard those words from his lips." He said thank you once again for that beautiful gift, I was not expecting this he replied and reached over and embraced and kissed her.

While they waited Jalon proceeded to speak and call attention to what he had on his heart to talk about, he stated I called this gathering to finally discuss and clarify the situation last year prior to you leaving for the mission in Africa. Okay! Caroline replies it is still a hard thing to discuss at this present time, but I do know in order to move on it must be discussed. So true he replied, first I would like to apologize to you, and if I have deliberately hurt you in any way and ask your forgiveness! I'm sorry for your pain and hurt that I caused, I know you were hurt and yourselves I was not honest with you and you, and I do know, you were upset and that was one of the main reasons you left for Africa on that mission trip, because it was too hard for you to handle. I just spoke tears ran down her face and cheeks because it was still a very sensitive area to deal with and she was still trying to heal from the scars once again, he apologized and handed her his handkerchief to wipe away her tears. He said we need to put closure to this, this is the reason I asked you to come so we can talk but I also see it is hurting you. Caroline said yes! But it is okay, let us go on. We need and I need to put closure to this so I can move on. When you asked me the question, you asked me previously about what you heard I said yes! And the no! To the questions, but you only heard the yes! Heart and you were angry, and I did not get the opportunity to explain the entire situation to you. You are right, Caroline ex claimed.

Jalon, said Several years ago I was very young and naïve, I dated this young woman but while I was seeing her she was seeing someone else also, and gotten pregnant but because the kind of man that I am I was about to marry her to give the Twins my name and take care of my responsibility to be a father and a husband to them, but prior to us getting married after the babies was born I noticed a guy one day after work stopping by to see her and I and enquired who he was but she lied to me and on another occasion I noticed the same guy and I confronted him and he said "I don't know what she told you, but these boys are mine". A just wanted to do the right thing after I heard these baby boys could possibly be mine, I wanted to be a father to them if they were mine, because I did not have a father when I was growing up so after we talked, I went home and confronted her, and she lied again and told me they were old friends. He wanted a relationship, and I refused. So now that I heard the stories I believed the young man because no man would be crazy enough to take care of another man's children in this case, so I challenged her to have a paternity test, because if she had something to hide she would refuse so she did not, and we had the test done and when the test results came back it was negative for me so that the young man was the father of the twin boys. Oh no! Caroline replied, "I am so sorry to hear that news must have hurt you deeply and tear your heart into pieces, yes! Jalon replied she betrayed me I was very hurt so bad it took a long time to heal and for me to trust anyone that I had to depend on the Lord and ask him to heal me, that was one reason I never got involved or got married waiting on the Lord so he will find and send me the right person. I understand Caroline replied, now she was embarrassed the car she judged him wrongfully without hearing the entire story, please forgive me she replied, Jalon said it was a misunderstanding and emotional imbalance played a part in this I have forgiven you months ago, I was waiting on you to get over being angry so I could explain to you it was a miss understanding and also because of what happened I relocated here to start over to have a new start again Caroline replied, I am so sorry all to hear all that had happened to you. Now that everything has been said and exposed to and clarified can we change the subject asked Caroline to something more positive, of course Jalon replied. So, I see you are no longer teaching at the other church! Before he could answer the waitress brought their drinks and water and appetizers.

Thank you they replied to the waitress she said your meal will be here shortly, okay thanks again they replied. Then Jalon said, I said no to your question, now I still help them periodically, but as you already know I was in school and now it's completed and a short while after you left for Africa the Lord elevated me and a new opening came for a pastor to teach at this new church, and I felt led by this. So, I took the opportunity. I am happy where I am today. Caroline replied "I am happy for you also" not long after the main course arrived and was served, and it all looked so good they both replied, let us pray! So, they did, then Caroline said thank you for bringing me here, it has been a while since I have eaten Brazilian cuisine, you are welcome! He replied, as they dug in to eat because they were both hungry and had not eaten much all day for this occasion. It was well worth the wait, Unum... Tasty! "It is delicious," replied to Caroline.

Jalon asked, will you be distant, or will you give me the opportunity to call you more often? I truly want to stay in close contact with you and would like once again to get to know Caroline better. I hope this is not a problem and there is no pressure! "Oh no she replied, it is okay, thank you for asking! Thank you, Jalon, replied for accepting. As the evening and did and they completed their meals followed by dessert, triple chocolate à la mode topped with vanilla ice cream and fresh strawberries; that was great! They replied to each other. Thanks again for taking me out, this was a wonderful evening, I enjoyed every moment of it, then Jalon asked, when can we do this again? Caroline replied, "Give me some time, I will check on my schedule and I will let you know.

This was great he replied, and I want to spend some time with you and do this again, this was truly great! The evening ended and he brought her home, they embraced each other with a beautiful hug, and he kissed her on the cheek's goodbye, he opened the car door and escorted her up on the porch and waited until she opened the front door. Good night once again he replied to good night then she replied and said once again it was a great evening, I had a wonderful time, which is great I am happy you did. Caroline waved goodbye as she entered her door, and Jalon went to his car while she watched until he drove away.

As soon as he reached home, he called her and let her know you made it home safely, that is good she replied, I know it's getting late, and I know you need your rest I won't hold you for long and if it's God's we will talk tomorrow! Thanks for calling and have a good night's rest, then she hung up the phone... Click!

As Caroline starts to settle in for the night, she reminisced on all that occurred June the evening, it was a great evening she thought to herself, it was hard to sleep right away but eventually she did. It was the same for Jalon, he tossed and turned and reminisced on the evening they had, the conversations and finally was able to put the past behind him that had caused so much pain and misunderstanding, then finally he was able to go to sleep.

"True happiness can be found
in the tiniest of things."
Unknown

CHAPTER 10

THE BIRTH OF HER GRANDSON

The next morning Caroline check her voicemail and it was her son Jeff, he left a message her daughter-in-law Lorie started to have contractions last night, she was in "labor "Caroline called her son Jeff to see how for a long she was progressing, and if they are at home or at the hospital, he replied she's progress thing well about 2 centimeters and we just got to the hospital, Caroline was so excited and happy because this was her first grandchild. She got out quickly, took a shower and gathered her thoughts contrast and headed over to the hospital. I hate to be there, she thought after being sick and having such a long ordeal being in the hospital, but she knows this is a special occasion and must be there. When she arrived up to the maternity ward to the room where they were Jeff was holding lories hand and was help coaching her to breathe. His mom was proud of him even though he was a bit nervous, but he was very happy to see her when she arrived. This will be their first child, and they are happy and excited and nervous too. She kissed Lori as she entered and encouraged her that everything will be okay soon and kissed and hugged her son and encouraged him to be strong that everything will be all right.

After the greeting, Caroline came and sat by the bedside and held Lorie's hand to help coach her also with her breathing. The nurse arrived shortly after and rechecked Lori, she was now at 3 cm and progressing well! Lori refuse to have pain killer, no epidural she stated, she wanted to have a natural labor and birth. The nurse gave her ice chips to help with her thirst and dry mouth, she was already prepped and ready to go.

Caroline was happy! Because everything was progressing well without complications, she prayed to the Lord Lori was now feeling intense pressure and pain, but she was a" trooper." I am very strong woman and was breathing through the pain. Caroline encourages her "you are doing good Lori; you are doing a great job keep it up, just breathe through the pain and focus on seeing the face of that beautiful baby that you're about to hold in your arms." Okay she replied as she felt a contraction coming and she breathed through the pain. Finally, Lori's parents and sister arrived at the hospital after a long trip out of town, but they made it just in time before she gives birth. The hugged and kissed her quickly before the next contraction arrived and encouraged her to breathe and that they were there for her while her father stepped out into the waiting room while mom and sister stayed and supported her, they hugged and encourage Jeff their son-in-law and greeted his mother and support each other throughout the labor process. As they positioned themselves for the birth of their first grandchild, they were all excited, her mom wiped her forehead as she sweat from breathing, and her sister coached her along during the contractions to breathe.

The nurse arrived once again and rechecked her and she was now 8 cm dilation, the doctor arrived shortly after and rechecked and examined her she was dilating fast, and he was almost time to start pushing! The doctor stayed close by and paid close attention to the rechecked a short while later and she was now at 10 cm it was time to push he stated, he gave her instructions and how to breathe and push when she felt the contractions coming! The nurse was there to assist them with his gown, and gloves etc. The Dr. rechecked again, and she was fully dilated and was ready to go. They once again encouraged her to bring in and out and pushed when she felt the next contraction on arrival. Her husband was excited, and nervous they were all happy to hear the good news, as she pushed, he whispered in her ears and tell her how much he loved her and encourage her to push as he held her hand and at times wiped away the sweat from her forehead, and the contraction arrived they yelled "PUSH". After about 10 minutes of hard labor and contractions she finally gave birth to a baby boy! They clean them up quickly and gave him directly to Lori by putting them on her chest she held and kissed his face for a moment cried a bit then gave him to his father. Then to Caroline who did the same and passed them around to the in-laws.

"Isn't he precious," they exclaimed"! They all agreed about the name, and they named him "Samuel" because he was a blessing and a miracle that came at a time to bring joy after so many tragedies. They were proud parents of a healthy 10-pound baby boy there was laughter now and smiled all around, Caroline was now a proud grandmother she smiled as she held him once again in her arms and now forgotten her ordeal she had been through a few weeks' prior in the same hospital, she too needed a few moments of privacy outside in the waiting area while she called Jalon and told him the good news! Congratulations he replied, I am so elated and happy for you, thanks she replied, we will talk again soon okay, soon he replied, and hung up, she now called her friend Pam and told her the good news, "hello Pam my daughter in law Lori just had the baby" that is great news she replied, why did she have? Caroline replied with a 10-pound help to the handsome baby boy! They named him Samuel, how is Lori she asked, she replied Lori is a trooper she is doing wonderful, just great, she's doing just great thanks for asking. Pardon my manners Caroline replied with excitement "I forgot to ask you how you are doing, and stated she was doing good, and how are you Pam asks! Caroline replied I am doing great I could not ask for better, I tried not to dwell on what happened weeks ago thank God I am alive to see the birth of my first grandchild, thank you for asking. Pam replied to a man on that! I am happy to hear you are doing well thanks for calling and sharing the good news, will I see you on Sunday at church she asked? Caroline replied I will pray about it and see how the spirit leads me, but I do believe it is a strong possibility, okay Pam replied, by I the way I will stop by okay! See you soon, bye for now, and Hong up.

Then Caroline slowly walked back into the room with a smile on her face, they were all in Congress aiding and holding the baby. How do you feel Caroline ask Lori how she feels? She stated I feel good, good to be a grandmother, how are you feeling Lori after this ordeal Caroline ask! She stated much better it is now over but a bit exhausted, thank God. A short while later Caroline kissed Lori and the grand baby and her son and the in-laws and said goodbye for the evening so Lori could get some rest, "I will see you tomorrow she replied. But her husband stayed by her side while she took a nap, and he tended to his son. While the family stayed a while in the waiting room, but they walked.

Caroline went to the elevator and talked with her for a while about how she was feeling after her ordeal for her life and surgery. Then Caroline asks "So where are you staying? They replied they were staying with some relatives the next town over from the hospital, okay she replied, before you leave let us plan to spend some time together okay and they replied yes! We will let you know! Hopefully, we will see each other tomorrow when we come back to visit. They embraced and said goodbye and took the elevator and went back upstairs into the waiting room, so this could spend a little bit more time with their daughter Lori and the new grandbaby. While Caroline walked across the parking lot towards her car and headed towards home.

Caroline was a bit tired herself, so as soon as possible she got home she had a sandwich for dinner and went to bed, because she was at the hospital all day and it was now late in the evening. She was exhausted and slept on till morning, she was so tired she did not hear the alarm she said to wake her up two hours prior because if she slept too long, she would not have been able to go back to sleep during the night, but instead she slept through the night until morning.

The next day she revisited her daughter-in-law Laurie, and she was doing much better good morning she said! And Lauri and Jeff replied to good morning, she was well rested, but her son Jeff was tired, nodding away, he was trying to adjust to the new baby, by staying up all night, he was very tired, and his mom told him it was okay to go home take a shower get something to eat and get some rest. He kissed his son, wife Lauri and mom goodbye and headed towards the door. Have you already eaten; Caroline asks! No! Lori replied, thank you I am start, I brought you some breakfast Caroline said, and Lori ate in a hurry because she was hungry, a short while later the hospital breakfast tray arrived, she looked at it and picked through for what she wanted, while Caroline held and kissed her grandson. The doctors arrived a short time later and gave her the good news that all is well, and she will be discharged tomorrow for home, that's great news she replied they were both happy and excited. Caroline gave Lori a little motherly advice that will help new parents, she said, "you sleep when the baby sleeps, so you will not be as tired. And as he gets older start breaking him out of being up at nights, keep him awake during the days so at nights he will be tired and adjusted to sleep at night, he will also get used to days versus nights." Thank you, Caroline Lori, replied. That is very helpful! Then Caroline asks, "did your parents stop by yet? No! Lori replied, they will be here later because they stayed late last night. Okay Caroline replied. Later on, that afternoon Laura called her husband and told him that she would be arriving home tomorrow. Caroline stayed a few hours with Lori and then said goodbye and went home. While she was leaving Lori's family was arriving hello and good afternoon, they replied to each other and embraced each other with hugs and kisses by the elevator. Here is my phone number I forgot to give to you yesterday, call me so we can get together! Okay! Thank you, we will talk again soon. Bye for now, have a great afternoon.

As soon as she arrived home and pulled out into her driveway, Pam was arriving also, they greeted each other and chat for a while, she dropped off a gift for the grandbaby, thank you Pam how nice Caroline replied I am not staying long hair and stated, just wanted to stop by to drop this present off for the baby, congratulations once again on your new grandbaby! And of course, I am happy to see you too, she replied and smiled. "Wait a moment," said Caroline I have almost forgotten; I took some pictures of the baby looking at this handsome boy! Oh yes! Pam said he is beautiful, he looks like both of his parents, yes, I think so, said Caroline, their features usually change as they get older, that is true replied Pam. Thanks for showing me those pictures you are well, replied to Caroline. Pam said I must go now, sorry for the short visit, she hugged and kissed

Caroline goodbye. It is okay, I understand replied Caroline, we will see each other soon, I will let you know about church goodbye once again thanks for coming, as she walked to her car and drove away. Caroline opened the door and carried the bag with the gift in it and left it by the door, so she will not forget it the next time she visits her grandbaby. A few hours later there was a knock on the door, the doorbell rang, and Caroline answered it, it was Jalon, hello he said, how are you and hugged her! I am fine thanking you she replied and you doing well, he replied, may I come in? Yes, absolutely, come in and have a seat, thank you he replied, then Caroline stated, I just arrived to from the hospital, I see stated Jalon I tried calling before I stop by, but it went straight to voicemail, I see said Caroline I believe I turned my ringer down and forgot to turn it up when I left the hospital. I just wanted to stop by to drop this gift off for the grandbaby! Wow! How thoughtful, thank you! Replied Caroline, then he said I was in the area I hope this was not any inconvenient time for you, no she replied, I just arrived home about an hour ago, please make yourself comfortable, would you like something to drink? Yes! What would you like to drink, she asked? A sprite would be great, okay and she got it for him, "Are you hungry she asked, yes, he replied just a bit hungry, I do not want to put you out of your way he replied! It is no trouble she replied I am a bit hungry myself! would you like a sandwich, absolutely! Ham or turkey? Turkey, please! She quickly made the sandwiches, one for herself and one for Jalon.

Thank you I have not eaten most of the morning and afternoon, I hope I did not impose on you too much, Caroline replied not at all, enjoy! As they sat down at the dining room table. Jalon says a quick grace, and quickly took a bite into the sandwich loaded with Turkey Swiss cheese lettuce, tomatoes, mayonnaise, a bit of salt and black pepper, black olives, sweet onions, pickles and a bit of oil and vinegar. It was gone within minutes. It was delicious he stated! You are welcome, she replied, "I see you were very hungry! Yes, he replied, I was very busy, and I just did not realize that the time went by so fast, it slipped my thoughts to stop and get something to eat, my focus was to get the gift and get here. "That is not good," replied to Caroline, thanks for your concern he replied. I am normally very conscious about the time, and stop to take a break and eat, but today it was just one of those days that slipped by. I do understand replied Caroline; thanks again for the sandwich I think that will be dinner for the evening he stated, because it's getting late Caroline, I must say good night for now, it has been a long day, I will call you tomorrow, okay she replied, I almost forgot before you leave take a quick look at the pictures of the baby, wow! Such a big boy and handsome too! Thanks, that is what everyone says. I must go now, says Jalon, goodbye as she walked him to the door and hugged him and he kissed her on the cheek's good night! And heading towards his car, Caroline closed the door behind her as soon as he entered and locked his car door and drove away. The next day, early in the morning the baby arrived home, and Caroline received a call from her son that they were discharged and were on their way home.

Okay, that is great she replied I will see you later this evening, bye for now and hung up the phone.

About an hour later she received another call from Lori's family, and they planned to have lunch together for the afternoon. The hours went by fast. They met and had a great time, Caroline asks! So! When are you leaving to go back home. They replied in another week, that is great she replied. Now that Lori is discharged from the hospital before you leave it would be nice if we could all eat dinner together, okay! That sounds great, her mom replied. We will figure out when would be a good time then. "Yes, ma'am said Caroline. It was a great lunch, yes it was good the replied. Now I must go. I have a few errands to run Caroline said, and she hugged and embraced them goodbye, I guess I will see you at Lori's later, yes, they replied! See you soon, she said as she walked toward her car and waved goodbye.

As she headed for home she received a message from Jalon. Asking her if she was available on Friday evening at about 7 PM? I will call you again later when I get home." I must check my schedule she said to herself. Now it was about three months since the surgery and both Caroline and Jalon were doing very well. An hour or so later, she returned Jalon's phone call, hello Caroline! It is good to hear from you, so what is your agenda for Friday! He asked "Once again, I am free replied Caroline, great! That is good, Jalon stated. I would like to invite you out if it is okay with you! What are your plans, she asked? He replied, "Do you like bowling?" Yes! "I love bowling she replied, but it has been years since I last played. But I do enjoy bowling! That is good to know Jalon replied, it will be fun to get out and do something different. We could get something to eat on our way there, that sounds great, Caroline said. Well, would you mind if I have pick you up on Friday at 7 PM? Caroline said, that is fine with me. I will see you at 7 PM on Friday. Thank you! Jalon replied, have a good evening and I will talk with you soon, bye and they both hung up the phone at the same time.

Caroline picked up the president Pam and Jalon brought for the grand baby Samuel, and shortly after she headed to her son and daughter in law's house. She was a bit tired from rising early in the morning running errands and taking care of some business, so she visited for a short while, she was happy to see that all was well, and they were home adjusting well! She was happy to see your baby Samuel and gave the gift Pam and Jalon brought the baby, she said and held the baby for a while and then headed back home to rest. She slept all the way through one till morning because she was very tired. The next day Jalon called and told her there was a change of plans for Friday, please dress formally and I will pick you up at 7 PM, okay, she replied. I will see you tomorrow!

Now Caroline was very curious as to what change of plans and surprise Jalon had for her, but she did not mind, she was happy to get out of the house. Caroline called her friend Pam to see how she was doing, and to tell her she would not be attending services on Sunday! Now that she was going out periodically with Jalon. Hello!

Said Pam, it is so good to hear from you! How are you doing, she asked? Just find Caroline replied with a smile, I won't be going to service on Sunday, Jalon invited me out and I don't think it would be wise at this time to go, that's okay Pam replied I do understand and that's great you are going out, Caroline said "I just don't want people to start gossiping like the last time, this way it will be better, I do understand Pam replied, but we will talk again soon and we will get together on a girl's night out! Yes! That sounds great Pam responded, have fun, you deserve it, have a great time and a good night, thanks for calling Pam said, as they said bye and Hong up, Click!

"Our days are happier when we give people a bit of our hearts."

Deb Sofield

CHAPTER 11
THE DATE

Caroline was so excited as she anticipated in her mind what plans Jalon had made, she could hardly wait until it was Friday, because it has been a wild since anyone invited her out on a "DATE," but she was happy too, knowing it was Jalon, a man with class and integrity. And now that they are past all the mess understanding are now able to patch up the almost severed relationship. She was much happier and Jalon also. It was almost Friday, and she was carefully planned day, she worked a half day on her business that day and once again made arrangements with her son and daughter-in-law and their family for an early afternoon get together for brunch before they returned home she ordered the food and drinks while Lori called and notified her family to stop by.

It was now 3 PM and they all arrived at the home and greeted each other, held and kissed and played with baby Samuel for a short while as they took turns passing them around the family, they talked and laughed. The food Caroline ordered finally arrived, he sat down prayed over and left the food because they all had a busy morning and afternoon and did not get the opportunity to eat a proper lunch or breakfast, so date quickly blessed the food and started to eat. As they dined, they laughed and talked hoping to see each other again soon once they leave. The time was well spent, and it was now 5 PM and Caroline must leave to get herself ready for later. So, she played a short time longer with the grandson, then embraced the family and wished them farewell, hoping they will have a safe trip home. Shortly after that she left and went home, she quickly took a shower and put on her makeup and styled her hair and by the time she noticed it was time to get dressed.

It was now 6:30 PM and she put on the final touch ups and got dressed. She had a few moments to rest, as she pondered in her mind where he was taking her tonight! As she pondered, she remembered this was their first official "DATE" their first time going out, she figured it must be somewhere special. As she thinks on it, the doorbell rang she arose quickly and answered the door, she looked through the peep hole and it was Jalon, "he's always seems to be on time she mumbled to herself "she opened the door and they said good evening to each other, with his left hand held behind his back was a bouquet of red roses, he handed them to her, she smiled and took them and said thank you! They are beautiful, she replied and smelled them. "I love the smell of fresh roses "and complimented him on how he dressed, and he did the same. He reached out and greeted her with the usual hug and kiss on her cheeks.

Caroline put the roses in a vase of water, but took out one to take along with her, Jalon, observed her as she put away the roses. You look astounding and your hair looks fabulous, and your address dress complimented you well. Now Caroline was wearing a royal blue gown with silver shoes and accessories. Jalon said, whatever perfume you are wearing smells good on you! "Well thank you she replied, you do not look bad yourself, you look ravishing Caroline replied. Jalon wore a black suit with a silver tie. Then Caroline replied and said you smell good to what are you wearing? Something special I put together he replied but never told her exactly what it was, she smiled and pick up she the single rose and her purse and they head towards the door, she closed the door behind her as Jalon being the gentleman he was already standing by the car waiting to open the door for her. She entered and sat down, and he closed the door behind her and went to the driver's side. "I hope you like where I am taking you tonight, I hope you will enjoy it. Caroline said, "Jalon you have exquisite taste, so I do believe will wherever we are going I will have a good time. Thank you, Caroline, for saying what you said, and having such confidence in me. He drove out of the driveway and headed towards their destination, as they arrived and drove up Caroline observed around her, it was unfamiliar to her because she was still new to the surrounding areas, and this was the first time since she been there and getting out. Jalon parked the car in the nearby parking garage that led to the elevators that took them into the hall. They entered the ballroom entrance they were escorted to their table and seated. As Caroline examined the intricate details of the interior of the ballroom, the detailed crown moldings in the ceiling, hand-painted wall paintings, the beautiful chandeliers, and well-dressed decor of the tables, she was impressed. Just at the presence and seeing the people.

It is as Caroline continued to examine the small intricate details of the crown molding in the corners of the ceiling, the extravagant chandelier hanging in from the ceiling, and the hand-painted designs of the ceilings. They were seeded at a small secluded yet intimate table for two with beautiful floral piece arrangements and the decor of candles, the ambience was very relaxing as Jalon held her hand too and asked if she was comfortable. Yes! Caroline replied, then she asked if he had eaten today, yes, he replied "a small portion earlier today "thank you for asking he replied. I hope you do not feel uncomfortable with me holding your hand! No Caroline replied. They dimmed the lights, and the candles were lit all over the ballroom, and now the live band on stage romantic, mellow jazz, piano guitar, and saxophone selections, as they get ready to be served dinner. Jalon said I hope you are hungry!" Now I am" replied Caroline, I ate about 3 PM today and now I believe I have built up an appetite, they both smiled.

They were served drinks and appetizers, and the menu was given to them for the main course there were several choices to choose from. While she was selecting from the menu there was enough time to talk, and Jalon started to open up to Caroline about how he felt about her once again. "I never knew how I felt about you even when you backed away and left for Africa, I have always felt you would have returned to me, I truly felt we were destined together, it wasn't destiny join us back and when the incident happened for your kidney there was no doubt in my mind I must help you, because you were a part of me. Caroline looked at him with tears in her eyes, by the words he spoke, I truly hope deep in your heart you are feeling the same way too." YES! As the tear welled up in her eyes, Caroline replied," I do believe the Lord has destined us back together, although I was upset with you, deep in my heart you were still on my mind and after we spoke at the dinner that day you took me out to talk and you explain the circumstances and the truth I was set free for my heart to love you and fall in love even deeper with you! Jalon, I know no one is perfect, but I also know you are a good man a man with pride and integrity, and I truly believe you will be able to love me as a man should, as God ordained a man to love a woman, I believe if I give you the opportunity you will love me, and I will have no regrets". When Jalon heard those words coming from Caroline's mouth, tears fell down his cheeks and she embraced him and said "I do believe everything is going to be all right" he pulled out his handkerchief and wiped away the tears they were both happy and was on one accord on how they felt about each other.

The servers returned and took their orders and brought fresh salad and freshly baked dinner rolls, they ordered a bottle of sparkling grapes for a toast to celebrate that special occasion of their love. "This is great Jalon, I had not been out and have this much fun in a while, dinner and a concert this is the first for me, I have done many things in my life, but this is new for me, it's different, but good you have great taste and knowledge of what a woman would like! Caroline says, no! Said Jalon, not just a woman, You! I am enjoying this too, Caroline replied. Dinner finally arrived as they talked and finished eating their salad. It smells great and looks good, let us bless the food and eat he replied. Do you like this music selection yes! Caroline replied, good music very mellow and relaxing, I needed this. Thank you once again for being so thoughtful and kind. "How about you she asked Jalon! Yes! I could not ask for better, live, and great selections. This kind of atmosphere that something to a person when you are with someone you love and care about, Caroline replied I could not agree with you more! After a while some people got up and started to dance because there was a room on the floor to dance but Caroline was too shy, she just looked on and enjoyed the music, the socialized with the couples across from their table it was a good evening and a wonderful first date, Jalon thanks Caroline for going out on the date with him, it's my pleasure she replied thank you for asking me. They could not end the evening without eating their favorite desserts, and as the concert came to an end it was about 2 AM in the morning.

It was certainly a good evening; I could not tell the last time I had so much fun, and relaxation replied to Jalon! Caroline stated the same, as they got up, they said good night to the couples across from them, as they headed towards the door, they wanted to be the last-minute rush getting out of the parking lot and the rush into traffic. Jalon held her hand as they walked out and complimented each other again on how good they both looked. They could not stop talking about the concert and how beautiful the performance was and how good the dinner was. They quickly rushed into their car and headed out of the garage before the crowd arrived, they were not too far behind them trying to beat the traffic. They will both relaxed as they continued to Congress it on their way home heading towards the highway. Thanks once again for those beautiful red roses Caroline stated. Then Jalon replied you are welcome. Then Caroline asks, are you always this thoughtful? He replied usually" I was taught if you treat a lady like a queen, she will also treat you like a King." That is so true Caroline stated," only a fool would not, you are a perfect gentleman." I tried Jalon said, I always try to make my lady feel special! "That I see replied to Caroline, and I do feel special tonight. That is great he replied, that is what I wanted to hear, so I did accomplish what I wanted to do, and yes, she stated. That is good he said. Just being around and with you is special Caroline stated, I know we have not done a lot of things together yet, but in time, I truly enjoy your company me too replied Jalon. They finally arrived at her house and he, being the gentleman that he is, always gets out of the car and opens the car door for her and walks her to the front door.

I know it is late, I will not hold you too long, she replied once again thank you for a great evening. As she reached out and embraced him, he did to her and kissed her on her cheek good night! He she quickly opened the front door and went in and slowly closed the door behind her good night as she waited goodbye. He then whispered as she looked through the halfway ajar door and he whispered I will call you as soon as I get in, she shook her head and waved as he walked towards his car then she shut the door, and he drove out of the driveway. She undressed quickly and got ready for bed because she was now tired. She waited about 15 min. until the phone rang and it was Jalon, calling to let her know he had arrived home safely. Once again it was an awesome evening, it certainly was what Caroline replied. Good night, we will talk more tomorrow! By for now they both replied and hung up. She rushed into bed and reminisced for a moment about the entire evening and then fell asleep.

The next day Caroline called her son and daughter-in-law to check on them and the baby, they said they were all doing well. How was the concert, they ask. Ooh it was great! I had a wonderful time, Caroline stated, that is great! We are happy you had a great time and enjoyed yourself, you deserve it, they replied. You will not be seeing me today. I am staying in just feel like relaxing and doing some painting Caroline said. "That sounds great replied to Lori, how are your parents Caroline asked, Lorie replied they are well, and they have not left yet! Thanks again for the dinner and inviting us over, Ooh I almost forgot they said to thank you once again. That is no trouble you are welcome, I enjoyed it and being together with the family. I forgot to ask Caroline stated, did you get all you need for the baby from the baby shower? Yes! Laura replied some things are double that is great, tell me if there is anything else you need for my grandson okay! Okay Lori replied. I have to go now, Lori stated because the baby was crying needing some attention okay, we will talk again soon bye.

That day Caroline received many more phone calls from the church family and some of her extended family checked in on her and she had the surgery. It had been a few months now and she was doing very well, she called Pam and told her about the concert and the great time they had together. Pam was a lady for her, but she was happy for both, seeing all they had gone through. You both deserve to be happy, you both you are both God-fearing and good people, I truly wish you both the best to come. I will not hold you long, how are you doing Pam Caroline ask! Are you off today? Yes, she replied. Are you okay! I am doing great she replied just a little bored at times, yes, I do understand Caroline stated. Would you like to get out! Not today she replied I have a few obligations to attend to today, that will keep you a little busy, yes most certainly she replied. How about next week, sounds like a plan and a very good possibility Pam replied, let us keep in touch to see where we are by the weekend. "Okay that sounds great replied Caroline. You know I am here if you just need to talk! Okay! Yes, replied. Then Caroline said, "Pam I believe very soon you will be in the position as I am, soon the Lord will send you a good friend possibly a Boaz someone that will love and care for you." Thank you, Pam replied with a voice of joy and snuffling as if she was crying when Caroline made that statement, "Are you crying she asked, yes Pam replied just a bit the word you spoke deeply touched my heart. Thanks again for the roots beautiful words of encouragement Pam replied, you deserved that Caroline stated once again you are also a God-fearing woman and a good one too, and you deserve the best, be in expectation I do believe he will be coming soon.

I do hope so Pam replied, but for now I will wait until he comes, the Scripture tells us that "a man who finds a wife finds a good thing." That is right Caroline said, so it is just a matter of time once again I do not believe it will be a very long, and Pam replied I will wait until he finds me! That is good, replied to Caroline, I will not hold you much longer, have a wonderful evening, I love you, I love you too and we will talk again soon goodbye, and they both replied as they hung up. As Pam hung up and meditated on the words Caroline said to her, she went even more tears of joy knowing one day soon she will find a special friend too. Caroline now pulled out her pencils and papers, and placed them by her Favorite chair, "the chase." She realized it was now noon and she prepared a quick lunch to take them to eat before she got started. The chase is her favorite place she relaxes on when she sketches, and reads, by the window close to the backyard. We are she has lots of trees and a small Lake where she can hear the birds chirping from the trees and look out to the sky and the reflection from the sunlight on the water.

It relaxed her so she can now concentrate on her reading and sketching, but today her focus is on her sketching, she is almost as finished and the closer she gets to end the happier she gets, that's why her focus is the finished the specific selection in her drawing. She spent a few hours without interruption on her drawing and sketching, later she checked her voicemail to see if there were any missed calls because she had put her phone on silent preventing interruptions while she was working. She had one voiccmail, and it was Jalon calling to check on her and to say hello. Now each time she talked with him and spent time getting to know him the closer she gets to him and the more she feels compelled to love him.

His kindness towards her drew him closer to her heart, there was nothing too good for him to share with her and Caroline feels the same. The fears are diminishing because he is open with her, he has nothing to hide, and he shares a lot with her. He shows her she cannot trust him by his words and actions. Whatever he says is promised he does it. So, her fears are diminishing and her love and trust in him is increasing. Caroline finally had a chance to return Jalon's call! Hello, she said to him, hello and how are you today. He replied I am doing well. Thanks for asking. I am sorry I was not able to answer your call earlier. I turned the phone on silence because I was sketching and needed to concentrate and keep my focus, Caroline exclaimed, that is all right. I do understand, replied to Jalon; they did get a lot done he asked! Oh yes! She replied, he said that it is good, so it sounded like it is coming along fine, Caroline says yes, it is! I am almost done! That is great. He replied. I am happy and proud of you! That must feel will so good! It certainly does, to finish the final section replied, and thank you for those words of affirmation and encouragement.

Then Caroline replied and said enough about me, how are you doing today? How is your day so far! And did you get some good rest. He replied I am doing well, and yes, I slept very well, I slept like a baby. That is, she could reply, then she mentioned the night before that the concert was great and dinner too. That was the most fun I had in a while getting out. Then he replied well, "I am so delighted that you enjoyed yourself, that is what it is all about, getting out and enjoying life with someone you care about and love! That is so true. Caroline stated, I did too! So, what are your plans for the rest of the day? He replied, well, tomorrow is Sunday, and I will be studying today to prepare for the message for tomorrow! She replied. Oh yes, I almost forgot, that is right, I have not gotten used to the idea. Yet that you are a pastor, and these are times you spend with the Lord studying. But going back to last night. She stated after we spoke it took me a while before I fell asleep. I was reminiscing on the show and event, and how beautiful it was, and eventually I fell asleep.

I am happy we both had a great time, replied to Caroline, "Well will I just wanted to return your phone call. I will not hold you much longer so you can get your studying done and message together for tomorrow. Okay! Thank you, Caroline, he replied it was good talking with you, likewise, she replied have a good evening and they will talk tomorrow if that is okay, sure it is. He replied, goodbye, bye he replied, and they both hung up their phones.

As the weeks went on Jalon, and Caroline got closer, they talked with each other on the phone almost every day, the upcoming weekend Pam and Carolina got together as promised for a girl's night out, they went to dinner and afterwards to watch a movie, they had a great time together talking and laughing and encouraging each other. During dinner they spoke about life's journey and its ups and downs and their present situation and hope for the future to come.

"You give but little when you give of your possessions, it is when you give of yourself that you truly give."

H. Jackson Brown Jr.

CHAPTER12
JALON'S BIRTHDAY

Three weeks later it was Jalon's birthday, and Caroline had a good idea of what he wanted as a gift, his birthday was on a Sunday, so soon after church services. She asked him not to delay after service, and he was to meet up with her at the small quaint but exclusive Italian restaurant just outside of town, he loves Italian dishes. This restaurant made beautiful homemade cooking and baking, Caroline chose this restaurant because he loves authentic Italian cooking, Jalon finally arrived at the restaurant where Caroline was already seated and waiting for him to arrive. As soon as he arrived, they escorted him to his table. Caroline got up when she saw him coming and embraced him with a hug and a kiss, good to see you. She replied and happy birthday l thank you! He replied it's good to see you too, as he embraced her, immediately the servers brought their drinks because Caroline had already his drinks knowing his favorite, some appetizers from the menu as they contemplate what they wanted for the main course. While they waited, they talked and laughed, then he stated I wanted to thank you for being so thoughtful, I was not expecting this.

Then she handed him a birthday card, but before he could open it, the appetizers arrived. As they talked and eight there was a break in between, and he would finally open the card and read it! It was touching and special, and within a small bag, there were two tickets to his favorite basketball game, to see his favorite team play. He was so elated and excited. Thank you, he replied. This is a great gift. This is the first time anyone has bought me tickets to see a live game, and it has been a while since I have been to see a game. I know I am going to enjoy this! He replied, "I am glad you are happy. I thought of this to see you so excited, that makes me happy. Caroline said. Then he said great gift! good taste! You have made my day and thank you for the beautiful card, the words you wrote touched my heart. Then she stated once again happy birthday you are a wonderful friend, I pray the Lord will continue to bestow his blessing upon you, I pray you will see many healthy and happy birthdays, I pray in time the Lord will grant you your heart desires, you are a good guy. I appreciate the Lord sending you into my life. I will not take you for granted and those were the words that Caroline stated.

They ordered their food and finally arrived, good they replied because they were hungry and "we only have three hours to spare before the game" will Caroline stated, so let us bless the food and enjoy so we can get going. Oh yes! He stated that excitement in his voice, I am surprised that is what I wanted. They had their dinner and a small dessert which consisted of a small birthday cake for two of his favorite chocolate. After words they headed towards the highway towards the stadium, but traffic was ruthless because everyone was heading towards the stadium, but they made it on time and the seating selection was perfect. The place was packed, and the game was sold out! It was such an awesome and amazing game, Jalon whispered once again thank you for a wonderful dinner and tickets to the game! I will never forget this. The game started with a bang! With this team behind but at the end they pulled it off and won the game. It was Shouting, laughs, and mocking. He was a bit nervous some at first, but he was happy at the end they pulled it off and won the game. YEA! YEA! That was a great game! Ye replied to Caroline I am glad you enjoyed it. So, they left a few minutes early to avoid the crowd and to prevent the traffic rush. On their way Caroline asked" how was service today I forgot to ask she stated. I got so caught up it slipped my mind. I did two replied Jalon, I was so excited about those tickets, and I was so hungry, my mind was not on the service anymore. But it was good, a powerful power packed message and word. The topic was" trust the Lord no matter what happens." She replied it sounds like an awesome message, yes! It was. He replied. How about you, were you able to make it the service? Yes, she replied, the message was good too, but I need more! What do you mean he asks, is the teaching there on a lower level than what I am used to? Oh, I see Jalon says, soon you will be where God wants you to be, I received that replied to Caroline.

The next couple of weeks Caroline and Jalon was getting much closer in their relationship, they talked every day and see each other at least twice per week, they discuss many things about the past, present and future concerning their lives. At the weekends they would plan to do some special things such as going to the movies, bowling, and visiting the museums. They do these things together because the relationship was getting more serious. They become acquainted with each other. likes and dislikes.

One Friday evening Caroline invited Jalon to visit with her and her grandson Samuel, son, and daughter-in-law Laurie. She called them and let them know she was coming over and was bringing a visitor. That Friday evening, Caroline arranged with Jalon for him to meet her at her house and they would go from there to her son's home. It was now 5 PM on Friday and as usual he arrived on time. He pulled out and heart in the driveway and got out of his car and slowly walked to the front door and rang the bell! Caroline hurried as she finished the last touches of her lipstick, she brushed to the door and asked who it was. You replied it is I, Jalon, okay she replied and opened the door swiftly, hello. He says, "How are you as she embraced and gave him a big hug. She was very excited to see him, and he reached out for the embrace he replied I am doing well. How about you, Caroline asks! I am doing well also! It is good to hear and to see you, then you replied and said I am so happy to see you too. And handed her a one stemmed red rose. Thank you, Caroline said you are so thoughtful, and kind. She smiled and gave him a peck on the cheek. She smelled it before she placed it in a vase of water.

You are welcome, he said. It was my pleasure, and he smiled as he stared at her, come in. She replied and took a seat as she closed the door behind her, then she asked, "would you like something to drink? Yes, he replied. Thank you. A glass of cold water would be fine, she hurried and brought the water and gave it to him. I will be back shortly. I need to finish the final touches on my hair. It looks good. He replied, thanks. She said it did not style exactly the way I wanted it. Give me a few moments and I will be back! Okay, that is fine he said, you can relax and watch television or listen to the radio If you desire, the remote controls are on the coffee table. Okay. Thank you. He replied.

he quietly sat and relaxed and meditated on the goodness of the Lord as he waited for Caroline, the peaceful and calm surroundings relaxed him until Caroline came out. I am finished she said, okay, it looks great I stated previously, he said. Then she said, yes, it is much better. You have a special touch I see, said Jalon.

Thanks, so Caroline grabbed her purse and keys as they walked towards the door, and she closed it behind her and hurried into his car and went on their way! It was a short time after they arrived because it was a very short drive to her son's home, about 25 minutes' drive from her home. They pulled into the driveway and as usual Jalon came out quickly and open Caroline door and shut it behind her, they walked towards the front door and rang the doorbell, who is it Laurie asks! It is Caroline, okay Lori replied and opened the door. Hello, they replied to each other as they embraced in a hug.

Then Jalon said to Caroline, "I forgot something in the car. Excuse me for a moment I will be right back while he went to the car Lori and Caroline talked and waited for him, he arrived and once again he said hello and embraced Lori and said it's so good to see you and she replied the same as she extended her arms to embraced him with the hug. It is a pleasure to finally meet you. He said the same here. She replied, then he said, congratulations to you and your husband and your new baby and he handed her a beautiful bouquet of flowers, thank you. Laura replied, they are certainly beautiful! And again, thank you for the beautiful gift you sent Caroline for the baby! You are welcome, Jalon replied.

It was so nice to have finally met you! Lauri replied! Then Caroline said, those are such beautiful flowers. I did not see them, they were hidden on the backseat he replied, you are so thoughtful. She said then Lori welcomes them inside. Have a seat, would any of you like something to eat or drink? "A soda and a bottle of water both replied okay," said Lori, coming right up. After she returned Caroline asked where my grandbaby was. Samuel! His dad is getting ready he will be out shortly. Relax and be comfortable. I will be back. In a short while, soon after her son brought little Samuel L, hello mom and Jalon he replied, how are you two doing it. So good to see you. Just great. Applied and he handed the baby to his mother Caroline. And kissed her on her cheek and gave her a hug he shook

Jalon's hands and greeted him with a hug. Then Paul said to Jalon, I know it has been a while, I have been so busy since the birth of the baby and since mom's surgery, I just wanted to thank you in person. I should have taken the time to see you personally, but I did not, I am so sorry. But now that you are here, I wanted to let you know I appreciate what you have done for my mom and me. My hat's off to you. You saved her life. Thank you for being so brave. It is okay! A lot has happened since then and I do understand you have been very busy, you are welcome, Jalon replied, with such humility. That is love and the love of the Lord. It is so good to see you. How are you feeling? Are you doing well? Jalon replied yes! Very well. He handed the baby to his mom. She kissed and cuddled and played with him. She was so happy to see him. It was a few days since she last visited.

Then Paul stated, "I heard you had a great birthday and how much you enjoyed the game," yes! I certainly did. It was great, Jalon replied it was one of the best birthday gifts I had in a long time." Glad to hear Paul replied. Caroline passed along Samuel to Jalon for him to hold. Hello, little man he stated and play with him for a bit then passed him back to his grandmother. Then Lori brought out some finger foods potato salad, baked beans, coleslaw chicken wings and more sodas and water for everyone.

While Jalon and Paul socialized about the basketball game, Lori and Caroline talked about the concert and the upcoming birthday and how she is coping with the new baby. Lori finally had a break to put the roses in a vase with water and Jalon congratulated Paul on the birth of his new son. They had a great evening talking, laughing, and spending time with the baby, after a while the men not away to watch TV. Their favorite past time was the famous basketball game. The evening was well spent and ended, and they said good night and went home.

Jalon dropped Caroline home, sat for a short moment and talked and then went home shortly after because it was getting late, and he had high respect for her and never wanted to be disrespectful or imposing himself on her. He left shortly after and went home, and as usual he called and let her know he made it home safely, so she would not worry. The next day, they said he was very appreciative that Caroline invited him to see her son and her grandbaby. It made him very happy and felt very special, then she replied. I bought you it because you are special in my life and my son needed to know. I do not bring anyone to meet him unless he is special in my life, and it is not many.

Jalon blushed and smiled and all he could say was thank you! I really enjoyed myself yesterday, and today I surely enjoyed the baby. He is a calm and quiet baby, yes, so they say Caroline replied." So, what are you doing later for about an hour or two he asks? Nothing says Caroline, would you like to go to the park? Certainly, Caroline replied, that is a splendid idea, it is now spring, and the flowers are in full-bloom, and they are beautiful, at this time of the year. I will also bring my book. Just in case I feel the urge to read, Jalon replied. I will bring my notes also just in case I need them. Okay, that sounds great she stated. I will meet you there! At what time she asked, and which Park? Jalon gave her the information and they hung up afterwards.

CHAPTER 13

PICNIC AT THE PARK

Caroline was very happy, because she enjoyed spending time at the park, it relaxed her. She did not know Jalon loved the Park too, now she realized this was another thing they had in common. They are very compatible in many ways, and the things they like. She was happy to see the compatibility between them, then she quickly packed a small picnic basket she had not used for years because she was by herself. Now this is the first time in years she has been using it for two. She packed some snacks, drinks water sandwiches and a blanket and put it into the trunk of her car and headed towards the Park.

She met up with him at one of the cabanas by the lake, where he was waiting and feeding the ducks. She snuck up behind him and covered his eyes, then he said this must be Caroline because she did not speak, but the smell of her perfume and laughter gave her away.

She released her hands from his eyes and gave him a hug and said hello, he smiled and was happy to see her, he kissed and hugged her. Then Caroline asks "would you like to sit here for a while "then he said yes. It is a great idea! Then she stated it is very relaxing here. Then Jalon says, later we can find a spot close to the water to spread your blanket, okay she replied.

As they were talking and feeding the ducks, they met a couple they are also feeding the ducks, and they said, "I don't know if you are married or not, but you do make a beautiful couple." Thank you they replied and laughing. Then Jalon said I brought a picnic basket! Wow Caroline replied, why did you bring she asked, he replied some snacks, water, juice, and she replied wow! Once more. Then she said we think alike! Yah! I see that is good, he replied. Well, no need to bring to basket. "We will just combine the food into one that is a good idea," said Caroline.

They chat and laugh for a while and said the ducks together, then sat back and enjoyed the beautiful scenery of the lake, then she got quite it and started to read then Jalon took his notebook and read for a while, then they relaxed and shortly after reading they ate and talked a short time more and then ended the evening. They embraced each other and said goodbye and went their separate ways. As usual when they arrived own, they called each other just to make sure each made it home safe. They both made it at about the same time and as Jalon was calling Caroline she was calling him at the same exact time, so she answered hello there we were both calling each other at the same time, she stated, that amazing he replied. Then he said I had a great time with you at the Park this evening! I did too Caroline stated, I thought that was so romantic a gesture of a picnic and bring in out the picnic basket, I do not think people hardly have picnics anymore, but maybe because I considered myself an old- fashioned girl. It is relaxing; I do agree with you, Jalon stated.

Hopefully soon we can do this again, I truly enjoyed the time we spent talking, laughing and relaxing together, I do too, she stated once again. Thank you for being so thoughtful and for asking me to come along. Most men are not like you, so thoughtful you are a great planner you think of things most women would like without asking them about it! That is my complement to you. Thank you. He replied we will plan this again soon! Yes, sir. she spoke. I must go now; I must spend some more time on my sermon message for tomorrow. Okay! Have a wonderful evening and get some good rest tonight. Thank you to he replied to goodbye for now we will talk soon.

After Jalon hung up the phone all he could do was reminisce about the evening at the park with Caroline and the good times they had. It was about a half an hour afterwards before he could concentrate or even meditate on the message for the next day! Caroline also took a while and reminisced on their time together at the park and what a fun time she had, and she relaxed for the evening and watched television for a while until she fell asleep.

Now it was about 3 AM in the morning when she woke up and could not go back to sleep, her heart and mind pondered on many things, but Caroline knew from her past experiences when she could not sleep, she needed to spend some time and have a talk with the Lord. She said," Lord, I know it has been a while since I took some personal time out to talk with you! I know that I should not let anything get in the way of our relationship and lately Lord, I do confess my faults. I have forgotten so busy, distracted the many things of life, you know what they are Lord as you already know, I just had my first grandson, a great friend and friendship, my illness from the mission trip. It has been a lot going on in my life lately Lord, but you still take the time to watch over me.

I am calling on you this early morning because I just need your direction and guidance. As you know things are much better for me right now in my life, I do not have to worry anymore about a place to call my own or my finances and my health is good! But it is one thing that I just want to be sure about the Lord, I do not want to make any more mistakes. At this time in my life. I am getting older Lord, and you have increased wisdom and discerning spirit to know good versus evil, but Lord, sometimes I miss the mark, sometimes I fall short, and mess up! And all I want this time is to be in your perfect will for my life. Lord, I do know you know my heart and how I feel towards Jalon, I know you do not make any mistakes Lord, I do know from what I see of him. He is a good man, he truly loves and serve you, he has a humble, calm and me spirit about him. He is very thoughtful and kind. when it comes to me Lord. But with all these things I do see. I just want to be sure, it is getting serious, and I want to know if he is the right one for me.

When I met him. I was not looking for a relationship Lord! And here I am now, falling in love once again and he is in love with me Lord! Please show me, so I will be in peace and know for sure. Thank you for answering my prayers"!!

A short while later she went back to sleep, it was about two weeks later Caroline had a dream about her friend Pam, and in the dream, Pam was getting married and I was her maid of honor, she called Pam that day and told her about the dream and share it with her. They talked over the dream, Caroline called Pam and told her "This dream means the Lord is sending your Boaz, you better get ready. Then Pam said I will be waiting and then they ended their conversation and said goodbye for now! We will talk again soon as they both hung up the phone.

"Happiness is having the right
person at your side."

Post Malone

CHAPTER 14

CAROLINE'S UPCOMING BIRTHDAY

It was now a few weeks later and it was Caroline's birthday. She was not the young chick she once was, but now she was more mature, older and wiser. A respectable woman in her community. She was now able to donate and help the local community. She was close to middle-aged but was 10 years older than Jalon. But look very young for a woman of her age. She took very good care of herself and health despite the difficult circumstances she went through. She ate well and watched her diet and exercise on a regular basis.

That morning, she received many phone calls and birthday cards wishing her happy birthday! Her son Jeff and daughter-in-law Lori called that morning to pick her up and took her out for breakfast, they brought balloons, flowers, cards, a small birthday cake and a gift. While they were on their way to breakfast, Jalon called and wished her a happy birthday and told her to enjoy herself and he would speak and see her later. She was excited to hear his voice, and he said hello and sent his love to the family. She opened her gifts, and as they drove to breakfast, she thanked them for spending time with her on such a special occasion and for the gifts. Her son Jeff spoke and remembered a few months prior. He said," if it had not been for the goodness of the Lord, his mom may not have been here today". So, they celebrated and appreciated what the Lord has done. Then Lori said amen!

The baby Samuel was growing fast, Caroline held, played, and kissed him, while he sat in his car seat. They arrived at the restaurant and stayed about two hours, ate, laughed, and talked. Caroline asked Lori about her family and how they were doing. She responded that they were doing well. Their time together ended shortly after. "Thank you! Caroline says I had a great time with you both, and I certainly enjoyed spending time with my sweet grandson. The morning was well spent and started off great. Then they brought her home. She exchanged kisses with their little family and said goodbye! Jeff assisted and walked her to the door with the flowers, balloons, and cake! Bye mom! Enjoy the rest of your day. We will talk soon. While little Samuel observed them while they walked away.

Caroline retreated to her favorite chair and threw her feet up and rested a while because she was full after eating breakfast. Pam called, as she sat down, Happy Birthday! Caroline. She stated I did not want to call too early to disturb your rest, I figured it was your birthday, so you probably slept in a little late. Thank you, Pam Caroline, stated, but now I have been up since 10 AM my son Jeff and The-in-law stopped by and picked me up brought me out to breakfast! And I just walked in. That is great! Pam replied, "I am not sure if I will be able to stop by today, if so, I will call you first. If not, we will meet up another day, that's okay! I understand Caroline replied. It's the thought that counts. How are you doing today Caroline asked Pam. She replied, "I am doing fine, thank you. Glad to hear Caroline say. I may be going out on a date. One of my friends set this up, it is more like a blind date. But I heard good things. So, since they went out of their way. I will go, I do not have anything to do today. That is great, Caroline said. Then Pam stated I was planning to take you out, but I figured it would be better to go another time because I knew you may have plans of your own, such as your son and daughter-in-law and Jalon. Thank you, Pam, for thinking of me. Yes, so far it has certainly been a good morning with my son and daughter-in-law and grandbaby. And that is wonderful to hear about your date, is he a Christian she asked! So, they say. Well just be careful, see for yourself and let me know how things worked out, enjoy! Okay Pam replied I will not hold you; you enjoy the rest of your birthday we will see each other soon.

So, Caroline went back to relax in her chair and stared outside the double French door leading to the patio area overlooking the small Lake beyond her backyard. The flowers were in full bloom and the birds were chirping, the sun was shining, and it was just a lovely morning. She said to herself," I could relax like this all day. I should do this more often." She stayed there for a while and gazed into the water as the sun reflected off it! And the clear blue skies. She stood and stared at the furthers point she could see in the distance, on till eventually she fell into a trance and fell asleep.

It was now about 3 PM in the afternoon and the phone rang, it startled her out of her sleep, hello! She said it was that familiar voice, Caroline knew it was Jalon! Did I wake you, he asked? Yes, she

134

replied I was taking a nap she says, I am so sorry to disturb you, he stated, I would like to stop and see you if it is okay! Certainly, she replied, then he asked do you have any other plans for the rest of the evening? No, she replied, what time is it she asked, and he replied it is now 3 PM. My Lord, she stated, the time went by so fast. I must have been tired and did not know when I fell asleep! Then she said it okay to stop by! "What time are you planning to come," he stated in the next half an hour or so! "Okay," she stated sounds like a plan, that will give me enough time to get myself together, are you dressed, he asked! No! Not for any special occasions, she stated. Then he said I would like to pick you up then Caroline asks, is the occasion a casual dress code? Yes, he says it's all right! Then he stated that it is fine.

I will be ready when you get here. Caroline said. It was about 20 min. later when he arrived, he did not live far away from her home, she heard when he pulled up and the car door was opened and shut, she was on the patio when the doorbell rang! Caroline quickly glanced into the mirror to see if her hair was in perfect order and put a fresh coat of lipstick on her lips, she hurried to the door and took a glance through the window. She saw his car and hurried to open the door! Hello, she said please come in. It is good to see you," he replied the same he wiped his feet on the door mat at the door, stepped in and closed the door behind him. Well! Happy Birthday! He exclaimed, "It is so good to see you. me too she replied. How is the birthday girl feeling today, he asks! Before she could answer he pulled her close and kissed her, and hugged her tightly, she greeted him back with the same affection. Then she answered . It has been an eventful day, I could not ask for more, it started off beautifully. I thank God to see another day! And Birthday. Then he pulled his arm from behind his back and gave her a dozen pink roses with a pretty birthday card and balloon. Oh! For me, she said, thank you for the beautiful roses and card, I do appreciate it , she was grateful. Then she kissed him again. She told him to have a seat while she placed them on a special table.

Okay he replied, you look great! You certainly look beautiful. Thank thanks for that compliment, you looked great too. Then she said these roses smell wonderful. You smell so good, then he asks. "What are you wearing one of my favorite perfumes, I will keep you guessing she exclaimed and smiled while he looked puzzled thinking of what it might be, he said he said OKAY! And he smiled and said you are a woman of mysteries I see! She came back and sat down next to him and read the birthday card. It reads," to a wonderful and special friend, a woman that deserve nothing but the best, may the Lord continue to bless you with long life and health, keeping you in perfect peace and gives you your hearts desires." Signed love always Jalon.

Caroline teared up and said thank you! That is such a beautiful card, and those beautiful words touched my heart , because they came from the heart, she hugged him and cried on his shoulder then placed it on her coffee table. Forgive my manners, she said. Would you like anything to drink? No. He replied I am good for now! Are you ready to go? Yes, she replied, and by the way you are looking good yourself. Carolines stated. "What are you wearing," she asked? It smells great on you. He replied one of my favorites. I will keep you guessing, okay. She laughed and said, "So that's how it's going to be? Yah! And he laughed, they both laughed. Let's go before it gets too late. He replied, she grabbed her purse and her keys and headed towards the door. She quickly locked the door behind her. He held her hands as she stepped down the steps and walked towards the car where he was waiting with the door open, as soon as she sat down, he shut the door behind her, and he headed toward the driver's side and drove away.

Where are we going, she asked? I will never tell! He replied! I see, she stated lots of surprises and secrets; Caroline said I will just wait and see, as he continued to drive it was a familiar road and she smiled and said, "I hope you don't mind," he replied, you have been here before, but you never came in. I hope this time you will feel comfortable coming in seeing we have been spending quite a bit of time together getting to know each other, I do hope your fears towards me are subsiding and trust towards are increasing for me. I would never do anything purposefully to hurt or harm you intentionally.

Now I am officially inviting you to my home. Welcome! He replied. "I am fine she says, and as he pulled into his driveway, she noticed the well-manicured flower garden and roses in full bloom, they were beautiful they caught her attention. They were breathtaking. The butterflies were pitching on some of them. He got out of the car and hurried over towards the passenger side and opened her door and escorted her towards the veranda and the front door. He opened the door, and an aroma entered through the entrance of the door, come in, he replied do not be nervous or afraid relax. He stated! What is that smell she asked? It smells so good! You are making me hungry. She replied, "That is good he said. He escorted her into the dining room. As she looked around, she said you have a beautiful home. Thank you, Jalon, answered. Have a seat and he pulled out the chair for her to sit and she sat down, she was still amazed the table was set fit for a queen. He had dinner ready catered for two, candlelight's, relaxing mellow jazz music she liked. a vase filled with yellow roses. He sat down and held her hands and blessed the food before they started to eat, then he served her dinner first, then served himself, it was the perfect atmosphere.

Wow! She said I was not expecting this, it is beautiful. That was all she could say because she was lost for words! Let us eat, the dinner was a mixture of seafood, Italian and Brazilian cuisine their favorites. Caroline said to Jalon, "I am so sorry I forgot my son Jeff and daughter-in-law, brought me a birthday cake and I forgot to show it to you and would like to share it with you! Okay, he stated and thank you for being so thoughtful. That is not a problem. Later when you take me home. "I will give you a few slices, which sounds great he said. How are you enjoying the dinner? She stated it is so good. Great choice! Thank you, he replied. I am just about full she said glad you're enjoying it. He replied. Then Caroline's said I have never experienced anything like this before, I truly appreciate this I will never forget this you make me feel so special! You are, he replied to her and smiled. I am full, she stated that it was so tasty and delicious. Then he said if you wanted me to, I would like to show you around the house! Okay, she replied he brought her upstairs and then downstairs and throughout the entire house and then onto the patio in the back yard where he also had the view of the lake. Then she said you certainly have good taste and it's a beautiful home. Thank you, he replied. So, they sat outside on the patio overlooking the lake and talked.

Caroline requested to excuse herself, because she needed to use the restroom, but she could not remember where it was, so Jalon gave her directions on how to find it. Down the hallway the 2nd door to the right. When she returned, he was still sitting outside on the patio as though he was in deep thoughts. She said, what a relief. I feel much better .

Then he held her by the hand and escorted her upstairs to a small room close to his study. There was a large box that was covered with a blanket, she was a bit apprehensive, and he told her not to be afraid to remove the blanket and open the box! She did and saw the most beautiful brown CHOW puppy with gray eyes! Ooh, my lord she exclaimed, how precious, he is so cute and adorable! Is this for me? Yes, Jalon replied, and she picked him up out of the box, as she picked him up, she saw a note and a little trinket case that rang like a bell that was attached to his collar, each time he moved it rang, the note said, would you be mine? She picked him up and kissed him and said yes, I will! stroking his soft fur from his head to his back. Then she asked Jalon. How did you know I love dogs? He replied I am very observant, I also had a strong feeling that you do, after asking many questions. Then Caroline continued to play with the puppy and embraced and kissed Jalon and Thanked him! He is beautiful. While Jalon stayed quiet, smiled and observed her while she played and opened the trinket.

Then she took a closer look at the trinket and finally opened it! And to her surprise "it was a" 3 Carrot Canary Diamond Princess Cut Ring, White Gold. It was sparkling from the reflection of the light on it. She was now amazed and once again lost for words. with tears in her eyes, she was astonished. Then she asked, "These are for me?"

He answered and said yes! Jalon was now on his knees as he took the ring out of her hand and said Caroline! Would you do me the honor of being my wife? Would you marry me? She was still in awe and astonishment; she didn't know what to say or what to do but she did feel peace within her heart to say yes. After she said yes, they both broke down and started to cry as he placed the ring on her finger she sobbed on his shoulders.

He said you are going to make me one of the happiest men on Earth! He embraced and kissed her, and she did too! I have waited so long for this moment; I truly believed the Lord has brought us together and brought you back to me and blessed me. I truly believe I found my wife and you are a good thing. I love you Caroline he replied, I love you too. She stated. Look how beautiful it looks on your finger! Yes, it does, it is beautiful as she stared at it in disbelief. She speaks. I was so silly I thought that the meant the puppy to be mine! They held each other once again, then Jalon said this calls for celebration. Let's get dressed and go somewhere. Go where she asked? I had no clothing to dress in. This is all I have worn. Do not worry, you will see. Then Jalon said go upstairs down the hallway the first 3rd door on the left look into the closet, there you will see something in a white dress bag hanging in the closet, get dressed and I will meet you here in the living room, hurry we have one and a half hours to get there. O my Lord, she said to herself this man amazes me. The observation the thoughtfulness. This is very rear you find this kind. She hurried to the room into the closet and found it, it was a beautiful red dress her size and her taste with matching pairs of shoes, purses, and accessories to match.

Jalon was ready and waiting patiently for Caroline in the living room, he was dressed in a black suit with a gray shirt and tie and shortly after Caroline was dressed and was finishing some final touches on her hair and applying her makeup to match what she was wearing. She walked towards the living room and Jalon complimented her and said, you look amazing simply put mesmerizing you are a gorgeous woman. I am so happy you accepted my proposal to be my wife! Then she replied you look amazing yourself and surely knows how to dress a woman you look sharp yourself! You have exquisite taste.

Thank you, he replied and took her hand and kissed it then held it as they walked towards the front door and closed it behind him. He hurried to open the passenger door for Caroline as he usually does and then hurried to the driver side and headed towards the highway. While they were driving Caroline just stared at the ring on her finger in amazement! All this seems so unreal as if it were a dream! All of this was happening so fast she is thinking "marriage soon! But she was very happy.

As they drove to their destination, Caroline stared at the ring on her finger in amazement and disbelief, she was quiet! trying to figure out where they were going, but the road did not seem as familiar as she initially thought. They arrived just in time and were able to find a parking space on the top deck of the garage, they hurried out of the car to catch the first elevator going down to the ground level. As they entered the entrance Caroline got a glimpse that it was an amphitheater and as they arrived at the door. They took their ticket and escorted them to their seats; the place was huge as she observed the surroundings. She figured it could hold about 30,000 people. She was quite amazed and was excited. She had not been in a theater like this one for many years.

Jalon, she said this is wonderful. What surprises you have up your sleeve! You are a man of many surprises, but I like it! You are welcome, he stated. Let's get settled and seated! The show is about to begin, and he holds her hand tightly. He brought Caroline to see a play, it was a play about a couple whose relationship was severed and broken because of unfaithfulness, taking each other for granted and lack of communication. The play started, and at the beginning of the play the couple blessed. They were newlyweds and for the first two years. They were doing very well, and they were happy! In their upcoming third year of their relationship was pure hell, they themselves did not know what happened, it happened slowly and as they slowly moved away from following the ways of the Lord he intended for their marriage and lives, they fell into the routine of past, Old behaviors, day in and day out, no more spice in their relationship that led to communication breakdown, then they started to take each other for granted and that led to one spouse feeling as if they were not good enough! The lack of attention they desired led them astray.

As Caroline watched the play, it brought back memories of her previous relationship and there was some pain that shook her to the core of her heart. As she watched. She said to herself this is happening every day in relationships. This is true reality; these are lessons to learn, and it is only teaching us to avoid these roadblocks in our own relationships. She whispered to Jalon, "this is a awesome play! I am enjoying it so far. How about you? Yes! It is great there are lessons to be learned from the play he stated! Certainly! she replied. I felt the same way too, I do agree with you. And as the play continued with mishaps in each of their lives, that could have cost them their lives. They realize that they truly loved each other. At the end of the play with some counseling, and forgiveness extended towards each other, with improved communication they were able to save their marriage and relationship, but it took hard work and trusting each other again to save the marriage. The play ended and Caroline was smiling, and Jalon was too. They applauded. He held her hand tightly as they walked out of the theater towards the elevator going to their car, they talked about the intricate details of the play.

She thanked Jalon once again for a great evening and a beautiful birthday! "It was the best birthday I have ever had", She stated, then he replied there is more where that came from! Wow! Thats all Caroline could say. When they arrived at the house the puppy was playing with its toys in the cage, Caroline picked him up, held him like a baby, and kissed him, She and Jalon sat into the living room area and talked for a while. What should I name him. she asked, as she pondered on different names that would match his beautiful little face. "Thats up to you," Jalon replied. It will come to you! yes, I believe it will as I lay in bed to rest. a name will come to me that will fit perfectly.

Then Jalon asked the question, now that we are engaged when do you see us being husband and wife? Caroline said, I don't know yet! I would need some time to think about it, and it also depends on what you are planning to do as far as the wedding Plans are concerned. Whether it's a large or a small one. Then she said "I love you! I have waited so long. We have known each other now for about two years and I almost lost you. I did not want to live alone for much longer without you." I do too he replied, okay, I do understand. She replied, "You have never been married before and I do not know the plans you have in mind. A small wedding does not take much to plan, but a large wedding will take some time. What are your thoughts on this?

She asked. It does not matter to me. It is up to you I am not bothered by these things when it comes to this. I just want to be with you he replied, and she smiled.

Okay replied Caroline. I have an idea how to arrange things. Once I sit down and put a little more thought into it, then I will update you on these plans and see what you think. What about children, she asked? I do love children! Jalon replied. I would love to have at least one, but I can't accept the situation for what it is, because I love you, but I do know this! God is able to do anything, there's nothing impossible with God. As the Scripture states, He will also give you the desires of your heart. "That is so true," she replied, I never thought of having any more children after my son was born. Okay! it's good that we were able to sit down and discuss this, says Jalon. Caroline replied. I do know that if I had the opportunity to get married, I know I would want a small, intimate wedding, just for close friends and family. Well, we have accomplished some things tonight. This was good communication.

Once again, I want to thank you for a wonderful evening and a Fabulous birthday! Thank you for my puppy, my outfit, and my beautiful ring. Well, it's getting late, and I do know you need to rest, please take me home so you can get home and get some rest! Okay! He replied. Caroline picked up her purse, clothing and Jalon picked up the puppy! Please help me figure out a name that is appropriate for him, okay, yes! He replied. Jalon carried the cage with the puppy and placed it in the back seat of the car and hurried back to close the front door, Caroline was tired and ready to go home. It was a long, but wonderful day, and she was very tired at this point.

She says to Jalon "I will also think of a date to plan our wedding and let you know. We will talk further about it to see if we both can come to an agreement." That sounds great! He replied. And she was very excited, but Caroline was nervous, because she was not expecting him to propose to her on her birthday. But she does enjoy the feeling of being in love and having someone who loves, respects and cares for her. She glanced at the beautiful ring on her finger once again and started to cry because the reality of being engaged and getting married started to set in as they discussed and planned a date for their wedding. Jalon embraced and comforted her that all is well and all will be alright. As he wiped away the tears from her eyes.

They drove towards her home and spoke about the beautiful evening they spent together, it was not long after she made it home and quickly ran to the door and opened it for Jalon to bring the cage with the puppy inside and placed it on the floor nearby Caroline bedroom, then she remembered the cake her son and Lori gave her. She promised him she would cut a large slice, wrapped it, and gave it to him, enjoy she said and gave him a kiss and a tight embraced. Good night! Thanks again for a great evening. She replied, "drive home safely and called me as soon as you get in, she followed him outside the door until he entered the car, she waved goodbye and he drove away, then she walked back into the house and locked the door behind her.

As usual, as soon as he reached home, he called Caroline, so she would not worry, and that he made it safely home. At the end of their conversation, they said good night! Caroline made sure the puppy was secure and comfortable, then went to bed. When she laid down, she could not go to sleep either, even though she was very tired. Her thoughts were on the day's events, she thought to herself. I have not had that much fun in years. I am so happy for the people who love and care about me, I am truly thankful to God for them. I am truly appreciative to them, as she looked at her left hand and observed the ring on her finger, she was still in awe that she was engaged to be married. But she remembered praying for clarity and confirmation from the Lord, and here it is! Thank you, Lord, for answering prayers. He is a good man.

She never expected or thought Jalon would ask her to marry him, at this time. Jalon, himself, was up for a while doing some studying, but after he was done, he tried to sleep but his mind drifted to the day's event also! And he himself was amazed that he was engaged to be married to Caroline, to him it seemed like a dream because he loved Caroline and had waited so long until this day. He never thought this day would come because he almost lost Caroline, then he said aloud "Lord, I truly thank you for this wonderful day and this woman you gave to me, she is a good-hearted person she is that" gift "from you to me. She is a proverb 31 woman you spoke about in the scriptures. I truly appreciate her and will not take her for granted. I do thank you for blessing both of us with long, healthy lives and for us to be a blessing to your people, give us the wisdom as we do your will and work for your glory sake amen." And the Lord helps us to get sweet sleep, and rest watch, and protect us as we rest amen.

They both fell asleep not long after he prayed. Caroline slept in until noon, but Jalon arose early for service, later on that day he could not keep it to himself any longer. He called two of his best friends and told them he was now engaged to married and a few close family members. Now Caroline thought about the date that would best suit them both to be married. After she got out of bed and pondered for a while. She called Pam, her best friend, Jeff, Lori and her mom Sabrina and a few close relatives and told them the good news that she was now engaged. Congratulations! They replied. We are very happy for you and Jalon! As a couple and all you have been through. You both deserve it.

"Thinking of you keeps me awake. Dreaming of you keeps me asleep. Being with you keep me alive."

Unknown

CHAPTER 15

THE PLANS

So! When is the big day they ask? We are still working on that, she replied as soon as we decided. I will let you know! Okay, that sounds great. Then Caroline called a few of their closest relatives also then later on she called Jalon to meet with him later that day to discuss further arrangements for their upcoming wedding. She was well rested and almost forgot about the puppy. She took care of him by letting him out for a walk and feeding him, I have to get used to this, having a dog "she replied. And thought needed to think through for the preparation of the wedding plans.

She did not attend service that day, now Jalon on the other hand, had to get up early in the morning and conduct the services, he had to prepare for the message late the previous night. After service that evening, he called and met with Caroline. She called first to confirm he was home and was up to discussing the plans they spoke about briefly the night before, she asked if he had eaten, he was home but did not had anything to eat the entire day, Caroline did not eat either except for breakfast early that morning, because she had butterflies, and was very excited, she had no appetite to eat, so she stopped and pick up some dinner for both of them to eat on her way there to meet him.

She arrived about an hour later. She pulled up into the driveway, while Jalon was waiting for her, he heard when she pulled up and went out to greet and meet with her. She brought the puppy that was in the backseat of the car, so he took the puppy out of the backseat of the car and Caroline brought in the food. Hello, he said, and she said hello! As soon as they set the food and the puppy down. They greeted each other with embraces and kisses. It was a beautiful afternoon, and they dined out on the lanai overlooking the lake. Then afterwards they went and sat on the swing close to the lake under the trees in the backyard, the birds were chirping, the temperature was perfect.

Jalon said, thank you Caroline for dinner and being so thoughtful! You are welcome, she said, that is the least I could do! While she played with the puppy by stroking his back while they talked. He placed his arm on her shoulders and said so what are your thoughts and plans for a wedding date! Well, I thought about it and thought it would be a good idea to do it at the end of the summer, possibly by the end of September, the beginning of the fall and not prolong it any longer than that! And that will give us enough time to plan a small wedding and get everything organized the way we want it. So, what do you think? Jalon replied that is great. It is perfect. Not too long and not more than 50 to 100 people close friends and family and to keep our budget to a certain amount.

That is certainly a great idea. You are a conscientious woman, which is what I love about you! Thank you, she said! Then he said we will be husband and wife before the end of the year. I am so happy, then Caroline said I am happy too! Now it is up to you who you want to do our counseling, and the wedding Caroline stated to Jalon. Okay he replied. I will get on that right away he stated, with a big smile on his face. I will also leave up to you and the color coordination, etc. thank you Caroline replied except the food, the drinks, and the cake, I would like us to be involved in the decision-making together for these and all else is up, to you. Okay, that sounds great Caroline replied how about the place for the reception? Caroline asks me if I will be with you when you need me to decide on a choice of the locations and what site looks best. I will be there to support you; I will not leave you hanging! He replied! Okay! says Caroline We are off to a great start, great communication and understanding. I will start looking this upcoming week. Caroline said. Then Jalon said I will do my part too! Then they called their family and told them the date had been set and it would be the end of September. Then they ended the evening on that note.

Caroline went home and called her friend Pam and told her the date and she was very happy! Then Caroline said "Pam we have a wedding to plan. I need your help and input and to help me! Then Pam said it would be an honor to help you, it would be my pleasure.

I am so excited for you and Jalon after all you two have been through. Then Caroline said, "By the Way, Pam, would you do me the honor of being my maid of honor! Certainly! With excitement. She said I am honored Wow! This was unexpected but great. Jalon and I have decided on a small intimate wedding! Wow! Pam replied, "that is great! When do you need my help, Pam asked? Then Caroline replied and said I will start looking next week, but for now I will tell you about some of the details, my color schemes, Coral, Ivory, and lavender. Oh, those are beautiful colors Pam stated. We will talk about it further next week. Then Pam said. Thanks again for sharing the good news and choosing me to be your maid of honor, no problem, Caroline replied. We will talk again soon, bye for now and have a great evening you too, Pam said.

The following week on Monday Jalon contact the pastor and friend from the old church. He used to be an assistant pastor and told him the good news that Caroline and he are now engaged to be married, and he is asking if he would counsel and officiate their wedding. Congratulations! I would be honored. He stated, so now the appointment was set for the first counseling session on that Wednesday at 6 PM because counseling was a few weeks and was prior to marriage. Jalon called Caroline and gave her the good news she was very excited! That following Friday Caroline started to make phone calls to find a wedding planner and coordinator and started to make appointments to look at some reception halls. On that said today she and Pam arranged to get together, Caroline picked up Pam then she said "let me see the ring anxiously, oh my Lord she yelled. It is spectacular, it is certainly beautiful and has a great taste! They looked around at several halls they knew would be a beautiful and ideal spot for a reception, but until I find the right coordinator I will continue to look around on my own. I want to see what they have to offer. Then they went to the bridal stores and looked and tried on several dresses to see the one is she wanted for her big day. It was a long day, but it was lack of funds Pam said yes it was! But I enjoyed the day and your company. Then they stopped at a small local diner on their way home and had dinner and talked for a while Pam says "out of the three halls we looked at in my opinion only one stands out the best. We will discuss the details. It was number three and Caroline agreed that she took the input of her friend eyes on details of that place, then she said we will go and look at three more halls the next time we meet again. So, Jalon and I will go and look at the final three and pick the best one and make our final decision. Yes! Pam replied that is a great idea, I am delighted to go with you again, then Caroline said "what did you think about those dresses. I tried on today?" Pam said, none seems to have impressed me and looked like the right one for you! None! Caroline asked, then Pam replied again, yes! None. That says yes, I am the one. Thank you, Caroline, replied. Thank you for your honest opinion. "What a friend is for replied to Pam, we will continue looking until you find the right one for you, the one that looks good on you, okay! Reply Caroline and nodded her head. I had a few telephone interviews with if you wedding coordinators and will be meeting with them on Monday for the next few weeks and months, I will be very busy with the wedding plans. Then Pam asks, how many bridesmaids are you planning to have? Only three bridesmaids and three groomsmen Caroline replied.

Now that you ask. Please remind me the next time we are in the bridal store. I would like you to help me pick out some of the latest styles and beautiful dresses for the bridesmaid and for your dress as my maid of honor a special design of your choice. Because I value your opinion and you have such good taste, I would like you to pick a special color as my maid of honor, to compliment the other colors we have discussed earlier. Oh, thank you Caroline for that compliment and I will certainly remind and help you of that. By the way, do you know and have already selected your bridesmaid, flower girl and ring bearer, yet? Yes! I had a few people in mind, have not called them yet! I am sure when I do call them, they will be honored.

How about the man she asked? I left the man up to Jalon to choose! That is a good idea Pam replied, seems like you guys have it all together. I must call and remind Jalon later to call those men and for him to start looking for their tuxedos. I have a" to do list" at home. I forgot it to be rushing out of the house. When I get home, I will cross out some of the things we have accomplished today. That is good, Pam said that will help you to be more organized and make it much easier for you! "Yes, ma'am, Caroline replied, they had finished eating their dinner but continued to talk and now ordered dessert for the road.

Caroline thanks Pam for the great afternoon and evening. They spent time together and then brought her home, then she headed home she was tired but excited. She finally named the puppy as soon as she got home, she looked at him and smiled and played with him for a while, then she said you look like a "Dexter" then she named him Dexter, she continued to play with him and took him for a walk a short while before calling Jalon. To see how he was doing and how his day was going. She also reminded him of calling the men he decided to choose to be is groomsmen and best man. And also, to select the style of their tuxedos and to have their measurements done, thank you. He replied to Caroline to remind me, but I was working on those things today! That is great to hear. She said have you eaten today? Yes! I had something like to eat again thank you for asking and being the kind, loving and considerate woman that you are. You are welcome, she replied. They talked about their day briefly then she said I named the puppy is name is Dexter, which is great he replied that is a nice name for a dog, it seems to fit him. Then shortly after she said she was tired and was going to get some rest and take a short nap! Okay he replied. I will to him a bit tired myself. We will talk later goodbye for now!

The weekend went by quickly and it was now Monday once again, Caroline finally met with the coordinators and checked out their portfolios, she was very impressed and was able to make a final decision and choose one of the four coordinators, she was happy and was not able to cross this accomplishment of her to do list, she said to herself. This will be much easier now that I found a coordinator and will take a lot of pressure off of me. She used the afternoon to view some online wedding band for her soon-to-be husband, but was not able to find anything suitable for him, according to her taste and standards Caroline is a sort of old-fashioned/old-school and is a very romantic woman she rather go into the stores and look for a band with Jalon and spend some quality time with him, so she called him and asked if he was available to go out for a few hours that evening, he was available and she picked him up and they went to the mall and some other exclusive outside jewelers and designers and he handpicked and tried on several rings that they both liked, and a decision was made for the purchase, and Chelan tried on the rings he could hardly believe he was about to get married soon he was nervous but yet excited at the same time.

Caroline was also as nervous and excited too, she yourself could hardly believe they were engaged and were planning to get married, the ring we had chosen is beautiful as they talked with each other. I do agree, replied to Jalon I am so happy. Caroline, you made me happy! Come here and pulled her close and kissed her, I am so glad you called and stopped by you have been very busy and I missed you, it has been two days. I have not seen you; it has been that long? she asked. Yes! He replied. I count the days that we are a part, Wow! She replied to it did not seem that long, yes, the days do go by fast, it seems when you are in love Ah, she laughed, then he said, let us find a place here to eat. I am getting hungry. She said I did not have much time to myself today to eat. That is the first Jalon stated number.

Then you are the one who gets the time to eat right, absolutely. She stated but today was one of those busy days that offset my schedule timetable to eat.

As they sat down to eat. Caroline elaborated on what she has accomplished so far, and Jalon was very proud of her, because he knows he had a woman who knows how to budget and spend wisely, she reminds him of that "Proverb 31 woman". While they waited to be served Jalon talked about their first counseling session and asked Caroline how she felt about the first upcoming session and their homework and questions they must answer and complete prior to the session. She paused for a moment and thought! Well! It is different from times past when I got married, all those years ago, but it is good, it makes us more aware of things to ask and to expect things that you would not normally think about and also if some things are not right and cannot be resolved by mutual agreement, it gives a person the opportunity to back out before they get into marriage. "That is so true he replied then their orders finally arrived, and they ate until they were satisfied.

How is little Dexter? He asked, she replied he is doing well. He is so fat he loves to eat and play he is growing fast, that is. He said he seems very happy with him, yes, I am Caroline replied, he is a good dog, he barks at night as soon as he hears anything to keep me alert. That is great! Thank you she says for purchasing him for me, He is a big company in a quite lonesome house, you're welcome! There is one big question I forgot to ask. What is that he replied! How are we going to do this, we have two homes, which one are we going to live in? That is easy Caroline replied, you are the husband your home is the one, it is the largest and the most beautiful of the two, what I will do is possibly rent it out or I will most likely give my son and daughter-in-law to live in. If they choose to do so. "This is a great idea," he replied.

They had dessert to go, because they still had a few things to accomplish before the end of the day, they left the mall and headed home, while she was driving. He made a few phone calls asking his best friend to be his "best man" and another friend, and two of his brothers to take part in their wedding they all gladly accepted and was very excited for them. Caroline was happy to hear the good news and told Jalon when she reached home, she had to do the same. Everything was falling into place. Thank the Lord, she replied. Jalon arrived home and Caroline hugged and kissed him goodbye, I will call you later! Ok, I love you! Me too, he replied. I had a great afternoon. So did I, she said. Have a great evening. You do the same. She said as he got out of the car and shut the door behind him and walked towards his front door and as he opened the door he waved goodbye once again, as Caroline drove away. As soon as she arrived home, she started making phone calls. She called the bridesmaid she had in mind, one of her sisters, and two nieces and the mother of the flower girls. They all accepted and were very excited for them both. The days went by fast, and it was now Friday once again and Caroline took a short workday because her mind was on the wedding and things she needed to do on her to do list was weighing on her mind, so she went ahead and browse a few places her wedding coordinator send by e-mail. She browsed through them and picked a few of the places and made arrangements to meet in person, she was impressed with two of the three calls and was very happy with her findings. So now Caroline has five calls and now must narrow it down and pick the three best ones so Jalon could come along so they could narrow it down and pick the final one for their wedding.

Now it was up to them to narrow down the final one. Caroline felt very happy, she knew that Jalon would be pleased with her findings, because she has good taste. Caroline knew now that she was almost done with the most important decisions she had to make personally, once she and Jalon make their final decisions on the hall much of the burden will fall on the wedding coordinator to do what she was hired to do. The only thing Caroline had to do. Once her coordinator contacts her it is up to her to choose and decide on whatever it is that she likes or dislikes. That evening. Caroline contacted Jalon and told him she found five calls and day need to meet the upcoming Saturday morning to view them to make a final decision as soon as possible.

He was happy to hear the good news, she also called her friend Pam and told her she had found two more halls and Jalon would be meeting her to use them in the morning and she needed to be on standby. That afternoon for them to meet up at the bridal store, Pam was so excited that things was coming together for both of them, their plans was falling into place, and she looked forward to seeing Caroline in the morning. After making the calls, Caroline went back home to rest for the evening. She was now tired because it took a while to view the halls, and she took some pictures also so she could see the uniqueness of each hall and what she was looking for to narrow it down to their final decisions. She did not have much of an appetite that evening, she had a meat loaf TV dinner and afterwards said and walked Dexter for a while then went in early sat on her favorite chair watch television for a while and fell asleep.

Early that morning, there was a knock on the door that woke her out of her sleep, and Dexter was barking and she got up to see what it was about and who was at the door. She realized she had overslept and did not know the time; she quickly answered the door, and it was Jalon. She let him in, good morning sleepy head. He replied with a smile and embraced her, then she replied pardon the hair and the dress, I overslept. I must have been very tired and did not realize the time. I must get myself together. Pardon me for a moment. Once again sorry to keep you waiting, have a seat and make yourself comfortable, that is okay he replied, I will play with Dexter until you return, Caroline said Okay! Sounds great, I will be ready shortly.

Jalon? Could you do me a favor I am sorry to be a bother, but since I'm running behind, could you feed and walk Dexter for me. She asked, almost certainly he replied with a smile. Shortly afterwards she was dressed and ready to go, you look beautiful, he said thank you look good yourself she replied. She hurried towards him and said thank you for taking care of Dexter and hugged and kissed him passionately. And again, thank you for picking me up! Have you eaten breakfast yet? She asked, no he replied. We still have an hour before we go, let's stop by the local coffee shop not far from here and have something to eat before we go. That is a good idea he replied. Then he said Caroline truly looks great this morning, you got yourself together quickly. Thank you, she said with a smile on her face.

Let us go as she closed the door behind her, Jalon quickly hurried toward the car and as usual opened the passenger side door for her and closed it behind her as she sat down. He hurried to the driver side. Then Caroline said so. I see you have been busy taking care of business! Yes! And you will realize further about me, I like to take care of business as soon as possible. I do not like to procrastinate. Why wait until tomorrow for what you can do today! So true she replied! At the Scripture says "tomorrow is promised to no man" that is right she said. As they drove to the small coffee shop. It was crowded and the no seating room, so they ordered and took it to found it quite yet secluded spot on their way to the first hall where they sat and ate their breakfast and talked for a while.

Jalon says Caroline I am so happy to see you, we do not talk as much are spent as much time together since the planning of the wedding started, but that is okay we are closer each day to be husband and wife, I cannot hardly wait! Yes! Me too, Caroline replied. Now they finally finished their breakfast and continued towards the first hall for viewing the entrance was very impressive, it is a nice place. Caroline stated, but I would rather you see it for yourself and make your own judgment. As in most halls the food is included, servers, tables and chairs, chair covers, tablecloth, and the DJ and these are some of the basic coverages in this package. They went through the entire hall, but it did not impress Jalon when he came through the entrance. So, they said thank you to the representatives that showed them around then they told them, "we will get in touch with you if we decide this is the case for us." They shook hands and exchanged business cards and brochures and said goodbye. Have a good day.

Then they went to the second hall and as usual the entrance was impressive. It includes all the same things as the first and was nicer than the first, but he wanted to see more and like the first. They thanked the representative for shaking hands and exchange cards and brochure of the facility, "we will contact you if we decide this is the place that through our knee goodbye and have a good day."

As they walked toward their car they talked about the second hall, and drove to the third reception hall, the entrance was impressive as the others, but this is nice so far Jalon replied. And continued to look through the entire hall. This is nice he says. Once again, Caroline, I like this Caroline also replied and she gave him a big smile. They went to the fourth and then to the fifth Hall and completed their task together for the day, Caroline said we will get together later on this evening and talked more about the halls and make a decision. I wonder which one we will choose. We will talk more later, Caroline replied. Once again, think about it for a while what you like and what you dislike about each of them and what you like most about the one that you like the best. Okay! He replied. He gave me a good idea and things I need to write down.

"There is only one happiness in this life,
to love and to be loved."
George Sand

CHAPTER 16
THE SELECTIONS

Caroline called Pam to confirm their meeting at the bridal store, she was on her way. Jalon dropped her off, thank you Caroline replied and kissed him goodbye. "I love you she says I do to him she replied. I am heading over to the men's department store to select the tuxedos for the men and for myself. Do not forget the colors Caroline replied to goodbye we will talk later, and she entered the store and looked around while she waits for Pam to arrive. Pam arrived a short while later and found her looking around in the store and said hello hugged and kissed her, so good to see you, I'm happy to see you too Caroline said to pam, then Pam says when I entered the store and saw you looking around I remembered the dream you had a few months ago! Oh yes Caroline stated I almost forgot, that dream you had was that was you the Lord was revealing it to that you were preparing to get married, and I was your maid of honor. So True she replied, I did not see this coming. The store attendants offered to help while they looked around, Pam assisted Caroline with the selections, there was a wide variety to choose from and some of the ones Caroline saw or liked did not fit as well as she thought. The attendant suggested she tried some dresses that are different from what she originally had in mind because sometimes those are the ones that will surprise you, they stated! Okay, Caroline stated and took their advice, then she said to Pam I am so nervous and as I tried the dresses on, I still cannot believe I am going to be married after so many years of being single. Well! Said Pam it is real. You are getting ready to marry, but it is okay! It is a good thing. Now Caroline is about 5'5" in height, weight about 148 pounds, where is about a size ten depending on the cut and clothing design. Shoe size eight, chest size thirty-six, waist, 26, and hips size forty. The assistant found a dress that had just arrived the day prior and had not been put out on the floor for display ads yet and after trying on several dresses, Caroline was getting a bit tired and frustrated. So, the attendant brought the dress to Caroline in both size ten and12 so she could try them on. She said, the dresses are elegant, and you look like that type of woman. Thank you. She replied to the attendant, these dresses on the hanger do not look like anything until a person tries them on, I agree Caroline reply. Thank you, Caroline, replied once again to the attendant for bringing those stresses to her. I will try them on my friend and assistant Pam will help me with them. So, Pam assisted Caroline by trying on the dresses and when she put them on. Pam says Wow! That is an elegant and beautiful dress and Caroline looked into the mirror and said, Wow! Herself. It is beautiful, this is the address for me. Pam replied, "wow! Once again, that looks great on you. It was elegant and beautiful then Caroline said I could not agree more. The store assistant saw it as she walked out of the dressing room and said wow! You look smashing in that gown; it looks like it was made specially for you. "I will take it "thank God I found the one! Thank you, Pam., Now Pam Caroline stated it is your turn to pick your address and then they will look for the bridesmaid dresses. They glanced through the many dresses on the rack and selected a few in the color and design of their first choice and tried them on, but none so far seems to look right on her. Once she tried them on, the color she liked they didn't have a nice, modern style, so Pam left herself open to see the possibilities of what looks good on her, the assistant brought out if you in her size and told her they are newly arrived also, she tried on an elegant satin gown with a 12- 24 inch extended train in the back, V cut neckline that extends off the shoulders, sleeve less, from the bust to the hips it was tightly fitted and from the hips to the ankle it freefall, the color were pistachio green, once she tried it on and looked into the mirror she smiled as she walked out to show Caroline, she smiled wow! Pam, you look awesome and elegant in that dress that color looks great on you. This is the dress for the bridesmaids. It brings out the beauty of your complexion, I know it will look great on them too. They were both happy and Caroline ordered the address immediately and scheduled a time for them to come in for fitting and measurements, then they continued looking through the many racks of dresses. They found the color Pam wanted but the styles were ugly, so they finally decided to go through the racks again and Wow! They said there it was a coral color, chiffon evening gown, strapless off the shoulders, figure fitting gown from the chest to the waistline, then free fall from the waist to the ankles, with a sash that hangs from the center midline of the gown to the ankle, with matching accessories.

Then Caroline says Pam, this is the one for you let us go and try it on. Pam agreed with a big smile on her face and said, wow this dress is beautiful, so she hurried into the dressing room with the help of Caroline, as she change into the ground Caroline fit the zipper up in the back of the dress while she replied once again, now that Pam had the dress on and observe herself in the mirror Caroline took a good look at it also. You look elegant and stunning; all the men will be definitely looking your way in that gown! As she walks out of the dressing room. It flows because the material was light and airy. This is definitely the stress for you, Yes! Pam replied I am so happy I found it, me too Caroline replied. You certainly looked good in it, and it certainly looked good on you. Thanks Caroline Pam replied with a great big smile on her face. Then Caroline shed tears of joy and thanked the attendants at the store and Pam for the time and the days they spent looking for dresses. They were done for the day and Caroline purchased that gown immediately. Then Pam asks about the Reception halls how things were going, she replied very, well, Jalon and I will be meeting later to make a decision on the final hall we will choose. That is great! Pam replied, things are certainly coming together! Yes! Reply Caroline thank God. Are you hungry, Caroline asks? No! Pam replied, "I had a good lunch. Prior to coming here and meeting with you, okay, just checking, thanks for asking she says. I want to thank you once again for coming with me and selecting these gowns and dresses and a short while after they left and were on their way home. Pam pulled up into Caroline's driveway and before she departed Pam ask God that you brought your gown are you nervous? It is getting closer. She replied, "just a little but I am happy, I never thought I would see this day that I would be getting married. I am still amazed sometimes that I am even alive and that the Lord has brought to me a wonderful man, such as, Jalon! In my life, yes! Pam replied to me since you a good man. Thanks Pam. Yours is not far away, Caroline replied. I can hardly wait. Pam stated. It is coming. It will be sooner than you expect, Caroline said. Then Pam opens the doors for Caroline as she carries the dresses inside the house and puts them in the closet. Pam had to leave because she had other plans for the evening. But Caroline surprised her before she left. By bringing out Dexter to meet her for the first time, she saw him and said, OH! He is so cute and chubby and fell in love with him immediately. You must feed him well! Yes! Caroline replied I am, I must go now! Pam replied, okay Caroline stated and gave her a big hug. Thanks once again. We will see each other soon; I will talk with you tomorrow. Have a great evening and goodbye for now and she walked towards the door and entered her car waved goodbye and drove away. Come Dexter! Caroline said let us go forward a walk! As she shut the front door behind her and put his niche around his neck, he was so happy to see Caroline as he licked her hand as she put a leash around his neck. He wagged his tail and barked pulling her in a hurry while he sniffed the common areas he marked on his own. She played with him for a short while, then went back into the house and fed him and sat down to rest on her favorite chair.

It was not long after that. The phone rang, it was Jalon's telling her he would be stopping by, within that hour, she was a bit tired, so she took the opportunity to take a short nap until he arrived. The hour went by quickly and it was a short while after seeing there was a knock at the door and Dexter barked and alert Caroline someone was at the door! Good boy! She said as she got up to see who it was at the door. Who is it, she asked. He replied to Its Jalon! And she said OKAY just a moment, and she opened the door with a great big smile on her face. Dexter was at the door too wagging his tail and jumping up to greet Jalon, it is good to see you he said and gave her a hug and the usual kiss.

So how did your shopping go with your tuxedos Caroline asked, it went well. He replied I found a nice suit for myself and for the men too, for my best man he will wear the same color as me but in a different style and the color to match Pam's dress and the other three groomsmen nowhere that talks, he does and the colors of the bridesmaid dresses to match. That is great, Caroline said, now that this is done, and you will not need to worry about anything at the last minute as it gets closer! Yes! You are right. How about you, he asks, yes! I finally found the dresses for myself. Pam and the girls. I am so glad that it is over, that is one less thing to worry about and I can cross this off my to do list. Yes! He said that is good for you.

Now before we discuss the hall, are you hungry or want anything to drink? Caroline asks to note he replied. I stopped on my way to the men's tour and had something to eat. Thank you for asking, perhaps a glass of water will do for now! Okay. She said, "I will get it for you. Dexter jumps up on his leg as Jalon pats and rubs his head, . Your water she said, and he replied thank you! So, let us talk about the reception, who out of all five we saw, which one do you think is the best? Which one do you like better Caroline asks, Well! Said Jalon, it seems to be gravitating towards number three. Well, me too Caroline said I like number three because it is unique and different in its sophistication. Now that we are in agreement and have the same ideas on the number three reception hall, they will now set an appointment to taste test a sample of their menus, I just hope the food is as good as the place looks. Yes! Jalon replied, because as simple as the taste of their food can be a deal breaker! Yes! So true, you are right she said but I certainly hope not.

My coordinator and set a date early next week if that is good for you? Yes! He replied. Just let me know! Okay I will. How about the limo service? Caroline, ask he replied do your thing. Pick what you want. I know you are a woman of good taste okay thank you the coordinator will handle that also, and let me know, she had a big smile on her face the photo and videographers my coordinator picked a few so we can interview them and looked at their portfolios, that is a good idea we will make a decision together. That certainly lessens the pressure on you Jalon said, it certainly does Caroline replied absolutely. That is why we hired a coordinator so they can do the footwork and make it easier and there is less stress and pressure on us.

Especially me, we know how woman worry about everything because it is our Big Day and be want things to be perfect. I know Jalon replied. Oh, I almost forgot Caroline said I would prefer a special touch in reference to the MC someone more personal and the DJ also at our wedding, Caroline asked do you know of anyone? As a matter of fact, yes! He stated, "I am glad you asked, I know just the right person for the job. Well, that is great. She replied that is all covered now. Then Jalon says, I will contact them as soon as possible.

Now I am relieved to know everything is falling into place, me too, Caroline said. I am glad they were able to talk and spend some time together. I must go in a short while, I must do some final studies for service in the morning Jalon started, okay! I do understand. Do you need anything before you go? Caroline asks, no thanks. I am good he replied thank you for offering. You're welcome! It has been a long week, and I have not had the time to see my grand baby, daughter-in-law, or my son. Because I have been so busy with the wedding plans. Perhaps tomorrow after church services. I will stop by for a short visit, which sounds great! Jalon replied, "I am sure they will be happy to see you, yes! She said I believe so too. I must go now! Okay, you have a good night, Caroline stated you do the same he said, and she gave him a big embrace and a kiss, and she walked him to the door, they said good night once again goodbye!

Then, as usual Caroline said do not forget to call me when you get in, okay! I will he replied. He entered the into his car shut the door waved goodbye as he drove away, Caroline closed the door behind her and went in and sat on her favorite to relax a while before going to bed. It has been a few weeks since Caroline wrote anything because she had been so busy since the engagement and the planning of the wedding, but she was happy getting back to her writing although it was not very long spending time writing. She was very happy and excited knowing she was at the last two chapters to finish. She stayed up for about two hours and wrote a bit, but writing took preference over reading ones Caroline the Picked up her pen she just continued to write, and it flows to was hard for her to stop to her. She had no writer's block it just flow.

It was getting late, and she finally decided to put down her pen, she was now exhausted from the long day! And now from writing though she enjoyed it and plus she had to get up early in the morning for church services. Now Dexter was barking it was time to let him out for his walk and relieved himself, so she let him out quickly and then gave him a snack and put him up for the night and then she went to bed, Jalon called to shortly after to let her know he made it home safely. The conversation was short, and she fell asleep. The night slipped by fast, and it was now morning once again, she was awakened by the alarm, she laid there and lingered for a while then got up by the barking of Dexter. She finally arose from an and attended to him before getting ready for church, Caroline decided she would now visit the church where Jalon was preaching now that they are officially engaged, and the news had spread abroad.

But before she got herself together. She had to call her son and daughter- in-law to check on them, because it had been about a week since she last had visit with them. Now that she spoke with them, and all was well. She quickly got herself dressed and ready for service, now this was a surprise for her fiancé Jalon he would not be expecting her to attend the services this morning and he did not want her to feel out of place on making her feel uncomfortable attending the church until they get married. But now she was dressed and ready to go, she locked the door behind her and went true to the church. The service was just about to begin, so she took a seat in the back.

Caroline is a woman who does not like to be seen or show off. She liked to be very discreet and inconspicuous, but after a while in the service Pam. Her friend noticed her and came over and greeted her and a short time after a few others. Then Jalon did too, he had a great big smile on his face when he saw her even pause for a moment and it now figured was a good time to introduce Caroline to the congregation and church family before, he proceeded with the service and will come the other visitors as well. He welcomed the visitors and welcomed Caroline shortly afterwards he called Caroline my name. She was nervous but she stood up into her seat, but he beckoned with his hands for her to come up toward the podium. She did and for the first time Jalon introduced Caroline as his fiancée and soon to be wife and first lady to the congregation and church family.

They were excited and clapped their hands and will come her and Jalon said a few words and then she went back to her seat and sat down. Shortly after she sat down, she noticed her son and daughter-in-law with the baby over on the other side and they waved to each other, she was glad to see them. Now the service was about to get started. Now the church was quiet, and all was attentive to hear the word and message for the day, while she was in church her wedding coordinator text her and told her the reception hall wanted them to stop by later that afternoon to case and sample the food and to select the dishes of their choice for their wedding. She was so happy to get the tax it was perfect timing. Seeing they were all together in church as a family.

An hour later the service was over and the people in the congregation hugged and congratulated both Caroline and Jalon. The service was great they replied to Jalon, "good word, great message." As he greeted the people at the door goodbye. Caroline was by his side, while her son and daughter-in-law and Pam waited in a seat in the sanctuary near the door until they were ready to go. Should the after greeting the last person will, Caroline greeted her fiancé with a kiss and embraced him and complimented him on how great he looks and on the message he preached. He complimented her also on how beautiful she looked. Then she talked about the new reservation at the Reservation Hall and afterword's she went over and kissed and greeted her grandson, son, daughter-in-law she was so happy to see them, while Jalon and Samuel Caroline's son talked about the wedding plans and how things were going and the usual sports. While Caroline, Pam and her daughter-in-law Lorie talked for a short time about the wedding plans. Now that they were ready and had closed the doors to the church, they drove two cars to the reception Hall. They were waiting for their arrival and when they came in, they were seated immediately and served them drinks, water, and the different selection of food on their menus to taste and to choose from the different variety was vast as they sat down and talked. The samples of the different dishes with their authentic flavors looked delicious. They replied yes! said Caroline I hope the food taste as good as it looks and smells, does everyone should know that a woman coming from the kitchen. Oh my God, it is driving me crazy everyone else agrees. We are going to have a hard time choosing which ones to select from the menu Jalon says.

I do not think so. Caroline replied. We will select certain portions of the ones we both like the best, this will eliminate confusion and stress. Yes! I certainly agree Jalon replies. Let us make our selection now and choose our menu now so we will not have to bother second-guessing what we already know now. Okay, Caroline said, the drinks are very good also and that is an easy choice. The desserts and the cakes were very tasty and flavorful. They finally made their selections on the menu on the selection of the main course. Caroline wanted and selected the wedding cakes and style from a cake magazine. They brought along to select from. Everyone was elated as they finalized it. The main courses. Now I am relieved Jalon replied to me to Caroline and said this selection I can now cross off of my to do list. They were all happy and excited about the choices they made, the reception hall manager was very pleased with the exceptional services from his staff and to see the customers' reaction they were very happy and made a quick decision.

They finalize everything signed in the contractual agreement and reserve the Reservation Hall for their upcoming wedding date. They ended the evening and said goodbye to the managers and attendance, Caroline to occur grandson Samuel Junior in her arms and held and kissed him for a brief moment, as she reminisced on the past. Once again how the Lord had. Her life to see her grandson Samuel Juniors birth and now her Boaz, the love the Lord had sent to her who put his life on the line for her and soon to be married. She could not help it. as she held little Samuel Junior closer. Jalon drew close too because of her tears. She told him not to be alarmed. It was tears of joy! Thanking the Lord to be able to live and see her family, friends, and this beautiful day. Jalon to collect his handkerchief and wiped away the tears from her eyes and her son Samuel hugged and loved his mom at that moment seeing he could have lost the only mother he had. They all hugged her and kissed her and reassured her that all was well and all would be okay after a while they departed in

ANGELA C. GRIFFITHS

separate cars Pam drove along with them. Thank you, Pam, they replied you are a God sent a true friend. You are welcome.

She started and they dropped her in her car. They kissed each other goodbye and said, "we will see each other soon call me later"! Tomorrow would be best, Caroline replied.

I had a great time. Pam replied to thank you for inviting me. You're welcome. Caroline dated by Pam said was the last time as she drove away. Jalon to Caroline puts the keys in the door, Dexter start to bark, he was now trained and was very happy to see them as they entered into the room he jumps up and greet them by licking their hands, Caroline let him out to relieved himself and to play for a while in the backyard. It was still early, and the temperature was a perfect 80° so they sat by the lake on the swing under the oak tree and talked for a while about the service and what they had accomplished with the reception hall. As they rocked back and forth on the swing, he held her hand and she held his. They talked and went into detail about the message he preached, the word of the day and the food they had chosen for their special day and the reception hall they chose for their special day and that they had made a good choice.

As they continued to talk and held hands. Caroline snuck in a kiss and a hug, then Jalon said to Caroline I have been waiting for one thing, you have not mentioned yet! What is that Caroline asks? You have been so preoccupied and busy this year, or mind is tied up on focusing on your dress, the hall. Then she said with you. Please stop putting me in suspense. What is it that I missed! He finally replied and said, "You have not talked about our honeymoon! Oh Yes! It is late in my mind she said. Then he said, certainly would not be as exciting without our honeymoon. Then Caroline said it would not matter where I spent it as long as I was with you! Oh, Jalon replied that is so sweet and I did not mean it to sound as if it would not be special. I am happy too, no matter where we spend it as long as we are together, but this puts the icing on the cake. I do understand, and Caroline replied. Thank you for reminding me. You are a different kind of man Jalon! Things that do not appeal or of interest to other men you pay attention to detail, you extend yourself to make me happy. Thank you, he replied.

Then he asked, "do you have a particular place in mind? Would you like us to go and spend our honeymoon? Caroline answered yes! Three places I had in mind, but I want us to pick a place we will both enjoy, somewhere you and I have never been before. Oh yes! He replied that it was splendid. I totally agree, so we are these three places you had in mind. She said the first place is Australia, the second place is Paris, France, and the third is Tuscany, Italy. Wow! That is splendid and quite a beautiful selection Jalon said, you have great taste, thank you she said what are your thought and idea. She asked, "Do you have anything particular in mind? Well, he said two of the three you mentioned I have in mind that is Australia, Paris, and Greece. Okay that is great. Caroline said Greece is beautiful and wonderful, lush, countryside similar to Tuscany, Italy okay, we both know the foods we love to eat! And those are just one of the reasons for choosing Australia and Parris France, but it is also beautiful too! Yes! Caroline replied, but I was also thinking about the relaxing countryside that we both love, that is different and it's our personality.

Jalon said OKAY that sounds great. Now that we know and talked about the destination. Let us look at Tuscany, Italy, and Greece to see the difference, which is. Two great choices. She replied and now it is going to be another hard decision to make. From the too! I agree he said and suggested that us look on the Internet and you, the Greek Isles and the Tuscany Italian countryside also see what it looks like, and then we will make our decision from there. That sounds great. She replied. Let us go inside and look! Dexter let go and he followed behind them wagging his tail. They sat down. Then she requested that he started the search, and I will be with you shortly. Let me feed and give Dexter some water okay he replied. Then she joined him. Shortly after as they both look through. They were both impressed with the decision they chose the Greek Isles and Tuscany, Italy. Now after looking at both the decision was much harder than they anticipated because they were both beautiful. It was a tough choice, but they must decide soon. Then Jalon said to Caroline, whatever we choose I would like you to give me the opportunity to make the reservations, okay! Yes, she replied she figured he had some things up his sleeve and some beautiful things in mind other than that she thought nothing of it because she already knows whatever he decides will be special and a nice surprise.

So, as they looked at these places and made their final decisions. They are beautiful places to visit, they said. he replied, you can say that again. Caroline said very nice. Very impressive. We will certainly enjoy ourselves; I cannot wait. She replied the same here. He spoke. They were both now excited and happy. Let us go outside and enjoy the rest of this beautiful evening. Let us go Caroline called Dexter and he ran towards her and followed her outside the door and throwing himself at their feet rolling around and playing. They sat under the Cabana this time because the sun was high, and they held each other close at Caroline later head on his shoulders and he gently massaged her head. She said now I feel much more relaxed and released, now that everything is arranged and is in place, we only have a few weeks left. But I will go over my to do list and just make sure we are not forgetting anything, that is a great idea Jalon replied. O let us just enjoy the rest of the evening I agree. She said we have done enough for today. As far as the waiting is concerned, again I will take care of the reservations for our honeymoon. I want to put my special touch to it Jalon replied, okay, great. Caroline replied.

"Love is always patient and kind."
1 Cor 13:4-7

CHAPTER 17
THE RESERVATIONS

Early that week, Jalon made reservations for two and put his special touches, as he stated to Caroline for their honeymoon package, Caroline also went over her to do list, and it was now complete. All the things she set out to do were accomplished. It was now completed and in place, she was so happy and was now a bit nervous, because everything was in place. A few days later Jalon received a call from his pastor and friend who was going to perform the wedding ceremony. He said, "Jalon we have some bad news, Oh No! Jalon said, what is the trouble?" There was a small tornado that passed through the town and a tree fell on the roof of the church and there is extensive damage to the roof and structure of the building "OH no he replied! all seems to have been going so good pastor Jalon, I don't believe the church will be ready for the wedding, but I have a possible solution that might be better that it's you and Caroline want to look at another church. A friend of mine has, it is an hour away from my church, ok, okay Jalon replied. I will talk to

Caroline about it, thank you! What are you going to do for services Jalon ask? Pastor Jalon, he replied to God will make away he always does! I will call Caroline and let her know what has happened and when we discuss it, I will call you and let you know so you can arrange the schedule with your friend so we can review the sanctuary. All okay though that sounds great his friend and pastor replied.

Then Jalon said auto my church is small. If you want to use it on certain days. Let me know and I will arrange the days and schedule to fit your needs until you are able to work things out! Okay Jalon, who is so thoughtful of you. Thank you, his friend, replied. I will think on it and pray about it he replied, God works in mysterious ways, then Jalon said and if I can help in any way until the insurance company pay to have the damage fix let me know. All thanks again he replied for being a true man of God! Thoughtful, that is what we are supposed to do is to help each other in times of difficulties and in times of need and testing. So true, so true, his friend replied. Shortly after Jalon called Caroline and told her the bad news, on know what she replied and all was going so well, I completed my to do list today and there was nothing left to be done. Jalon consummated her, all is well! Pastor said to talk with you right away there might be a possible solution if you agree! What is that she asked? A friend of his has a church and our away and wants us to look at it to see if you would like to perform the ceremony there! Okay! That is great. She replied. When can we see it, Caroline asks? Jalon replied. I must get back with pastor and he will make the arrangements as soon as possible. "Okay, sounds great she replied, then Jalon said I will call him as soon as I get off the phone with you and as soon as he let me know the day and time, I will let you know! Thanks Jalon she replied then Jalon said I do not want you to worry things will work out fine. Things happen for a reason sometimes we do not know why", I know, so true Caroline replied. As soon as Jalon got off the phone with Caroline, he called pastor and left a message for him to respond as soon as possible. The next day he had a date and time set for them to view the sanctuary and its grounds. Two days later they went and met with the pastor of that church and was not very impressed with what they saw. It was beautiful a beautiful, modernized church, Jalon and Caroline spoke with each other and the man of God that owned the church. He showed them around and that they spoke the thanks the man of God for the opportunity to use this beautiful place for their waiting. You are so welcome. The man of God replied. Then he said God works in mysterious ways, and they looked at each other and smiled. Let us go to the office now and give the details and date and time you need to use it; I can arrange for whatever accident you need on that day to open and close the church when it's over. So, Jalon. One being the man of God that he is said, so what are my financial obligations? The man of God replied nothing whatever the Lord placed on your heart to give us as an offering to be a blessing, especially to the assistant that will be giving a helping hand then freely do so.

Wow! Caroline replied as they looked at each other Jalon was speechless, all he could say was that it was a true blessing. Thank you! Thank you for your time. Once again and they made the arrangements for the date and time, it was perfect because that date was not booked it was available for use, very well the pastor replied the day prior to the wedding for rehearsal and the morning of the wedding for the coordinators and decorators need to come in to prepare and decorate the church. Okay the pastor replied again we will see each other then, yes! "We will see each other soon," he replied. They shook the pastor's hand and said goodbye.

Jalon's pastor and mentor was outside on the ground waiting for them, then he shook his friend hand and said goodbye. And they walked away and went their separate ways because they drove separate cars goodbye, they spoke for a moment before they drove away and said we will talk and see each other soon and waved goodbye as they drove away. As Jalon and Caroline converse about the grounds and the sanctuary. She was able to describe in detail the well-manicured grounds and lushly trimmed trees and beautiful flowers and flower gardens that surround the property the flowers were in full bloom with multicolored all it around to beautify the property and bring life to the grounds. The sanctuary. She described it as an updated mesmerizing modernized sanctuary with its multicolored stained-glass windows and when the sun rays hit the glass. The place is lit up like a Christmas tree as she described it with its multi-faceted recess lighting and vaulted ceilings, chandeliers.

The sanctuary is located on an incline(hill) that overlooks the ocean side. What a beautiful, and serene setting. It is Caroline said to

Jalon, all he could say was, yes! It is magnificent, Because the way she described it what exactly what he observed, and his thoughts was still on. The beauty of the place. We are blessed she said yes! he says we are look at the favor of God he replied, as they thought on the situation and continued to talk what seems to have turned out to be a tragedy turned out to be a blessing for us more than we had ever anticipated to have, so true, he replied. Then Caroline stated she would make some phone calls in the morning and change the address on the invitations and mail them out immediately. That was her number one assignment for tomorrow. I will call my coordinator and let her know the changes, then we will pick them up and she will address them and mail them immediately. That is a great idea Jalon replied. I almost forgot all about that! She jokingly said, "that is why you are blessed with a woman that is on target." That is great! He said and God.

It was now late in the evening and Jalon asked, would you like for us to stop somewhere and have dinner? Yes! She replied as they drove up to a nearby restaurant to eat. They were still amazed by this site and location of the sanctuary and the beauty they saw. As they talked Caroline reminded Jalon and said, we have four weeks left before the big day. How do you feel. She asked, are you at least a bit nervous? No! Jalon replied, then she said I thought you would at least be a little nervous seeing this is your first marriage. No, he replied, once again I am too busy and have no time to think about it, that a good possibility she said, then he said to her, how about you? Then she replied No! Not really. I am also too busy to think about it,

I guess. As the days get closer, I will be a bit nervous, I am so happy everything is now in the and it is ready! Me too, he replied!

As they pulled up to the restaurant parking lot, they ran into her friend Pam and a friend, Hello! They said as they greeted each other and waved to each other, and they parked. "What a small world," Pam replied as she exited her car to greet them, "What are you and Jalon doing on this side of town. She asked? Oh! They had some bad news and I forgot to call and tell you about it, as they greet each other. I will tell you about it later, Caroline said. Then Pam introduced her friend David and they both said hello and shook his hand, and this was Caroline, and her fiancé Jalon Pam replied to David Hello! Caroline said It is good to see you, me too Pam replied. Then they pardon themselves and step away from the men for a moment to talk what the bad news Pam ask? Caroline explained the church we were about to get married in got damaged by the storm that passed through last week, Oh No! Pam replied and sighed! So, will it be available and ready in time for the wedding? No Caroline replied, so what are you going to do for it church and ask? Caroline replied that is just it. That is why we are here. "The Lord always have a ram in the bush" God works in mysterious ways! As she anxiously waits to hear what Caroline had to say and said, that sounds like good news ahead, come on, spit it out please do not keep me in suspense. Then she explained and said, Jalon's pastor and friend that will perform our wedding called on another pastor friend of his that owned a church in this area, and we went and viewed the premises.

It was astonishing, she explained it was breathtaking! That is all I will tell you at this time! Pam said, Oh! You are not right, but I am so happy the Lord opened another door so quickly for you both. I cannot wait to see it! Then Caroline said on the night of the rehearsal you will see it. Okay, Pam replied. I guess I will be kept in suspense until that day comes. Then Caroline says I will be mailing out new invitations tomorrow with the new addresses. Do you need help, Pam asks? No! Caroline replied all is well. The coordinator and I will finalize everything tomorrow, that is great. So, who is your new friend Caroline asks the blind date, replied set up by several coworkers. He is a looker. she replied, yes but I want to see what is in that head and heart and here his conversation definitely Caroline replied! I would like us sit together, but since this is your first date we will give you your privacy, plus David does not know us so he may be a bit uncomfortable, I agree Pam said, I want him to open up so I can see who he is! I agree.

Caroline replied, "Well call me later and let me know how things went, good luck I hope everything works out well. I will Pam replied. As they walked back towards the men, they were standing on the side talking about the games. As they returned and met up with dates, Pam said it was good to see you and Jalon said the same and it was nice to meet you David Caroline and Jalon replied, David replied, it was nice to meet you both, enjoy your dinner then Caroline said thank you! Goodbye, and have a great evening. Hope to see you again, same here David replied. Bye for now and they kissed each other and shook hands and went to their separate tables and sat down waiting to be served.

Jalon and Caroline enjoyed that beautiful evening dining out! And talk some more about the new sanctuary and its location for the wedding. As the evening wind down, they waved goodbye as they left Pam and her new (Date) friend, they held hands as they walked out of the restaurant as usual as the gentleman Jalon escorted her to her seat to the car open and close the door behind her and then to the driver side way he took over the driving to their final this donation, he dropped Caroline off and kissed her good bye and escorted her to the front door and as she entered in he left, and as soon as he arrived on the called his pastor and friend thanking him once again for helping them to find a place so quickly for their wedding. It is my pleasure the pastor responded, and they said good night, then he called Caroline to let her know he made it home safely after a short chat, while she fed Dexter. They were both tired and he wished her a good night she said the same and hoping he would get a good night's rest you too he replied to goodbye I love you she said I do to replied to Jalon and they hung up their phones and went to bed shortly thereafter.

The next morning Caroline arose early to feed and walk Dexter, he was now a big dog, he enjoyed playing and fetching balls and Frisbees and was very smart, he was one of a kind! Caroline brought him back inside after half an hour walk and play. Then she said to him." Dexter, I love you, you are a good guard dog." As he looked at her as if he understood what she was saying, wagged his tail and as she rubbed and Messages, is head, back and stomach he rolls on the floor and then stayed calm.

Pam called Caroline later that evening and told her how things went on her date! She did not elaborate much.

Caroline was missing her grandbaby Samuel since she had been so busy and caught up with the wedding plans. She called her daughter-in-law Laurie and asked if she could stop by later that afternoon for a visit to see and spend time with the baby.

"A great marriage isn't something that just happen;
it's something that must be created."

Fawn Waver

CHAPTER 18
COUNT DOWN

It was now a week before the wedding and Caroline and her wedding coordinator and assistant went through their final list of things to do. They wanted to make sure all was finalized and in order. Jalon did the same on his end, making sure all the men had their tuxedos and apparels in order, and all was well. Now Caroline and Jalon were getting nervous with anticipation and excitement of their upcoming wedding event.

Caroline tried on her wedding gown. One last time before the waiting to make sure there was no final adjustment needed to be done, but it fits perfect as it did a month ago when she purchased it, no alternations was necessary, she called in her maid of honor and friend Pam, her bright made to stop by later that afternoon to check on their dresses also and all was well. She made an afternoon of a small get together luncheon afterwards at the house just for the ladies, now on the other hand Jalon best man had gained a few pounds and had to do some small alterations of his tuxedo and shortly after the men had a surprise for him a small bachelor party at one of the local sports rooms. Shortly after the luncheon at Caroline's home Pam and the young woman had planned for weeks to get everyone together for her bridal shower, everyone said goodbye after the luncheon, then Pam asked Caroline if she was busy after the lunch, she wanted to talk with her about her date further in details but would like to go at the Park to relax and talk.

She was happy and was in anticipation to hear what happened on their feet, because they never went into details about the date. Pam said to Caroline, it was too hot at this time at the Park, and they left she said I found a new spot a lounge I spent time together with some of my coworkers after work sometimes, it is comfortable, and very relaxing. Yes! Caroline replied, relaxation is what I enjoy and need at the present time seeing the wedding is just a week away. Then Pam said, so this will be a good place we can come and hang out sometimes when we are both free after the wedding, Yes! Caroline replied to sounds like a plan. As Pam drove and got closer all the family and friends were already gathered and were anticipating their arrival, some were friends and family already out, and were down on vacation for the week prior to the wedding.

As Pam drove up to the entrance of the lounge, it was one of the most exquisite hotels newly built in the area, this is new Caroline ask? I did not know this was here, it is newly built replied. Pam the expanded three weeks ago, Oh! So, it was clearly new, I cannot wait to see the inside, she said. As Pam pulled up into the garage, they walked down towards the elevators that took them down to the first floor as they walked into the lounge and passed through it. They went towards the back where they entered into a dimly lit hallway that leads to a double swing door leading to a room, this is nice, yet different Caroline replied as Pam let Caroline the way and pushed open the door in front of her. It was a bit dark and as she opened the door. They turned on the light and yelled "Surprise" she was in astonishment because she was not expecting this, the many familiar faces with gifts, boxes, and bags, there was a banner above that said" Caroline Wedding Shower." And had the date on it in her favorite color's coral, purple and green. The music was now playing, and they all came up one by one and greeted and congratulated her. Pam was smiling from ear to ear as Caroline looked at her and smiled, hinting that she was going to get her for this! And gave her a big hug and pinched her on her arm. "Okay," replied with a smile she whispered thank you! You're welcome, she replied that is what a friend is for.

Then Caroline thanked everyone and said this was truly a surprise, she cried for a moment, it was tears of joy! They hugged her and her, remembering the ordeal she went through a few months prior and then enjoyed the evening partying and having fun. Jalon also was having a good time with his close friends and family. The evening ended with smiles and laughter. They hugged and kissed Caroline and Jalon good night as their showers ended, Caroline could hardly wait to get home to call Jalon and tell him all that took place, and Jalon also was excited and could not wait to call and tell

Caroline about his surprise. As soon as she arrived home, she called Jalon, but he was still driving home from his party, she told him the news he laughed as she asked him, why are you laughing? She asked because I also was surprised by my best man and friends at a party! That is great. She replied and now she was laughing, that is hilarious, he said, and they both laughed together. I had a good time replied Caroline even though I'm a bit tired, but I had a great time. I am glad to hear that he replied I did too! Then she said I am happy to hear that! I am a bit tired of myself! Jalon replied, "As soon as I get home, I am going to bed, need too Caroline said. I would love to spend some time with you tomorrow after the service, sure! Get home safe and we will talk and see each other in the morning, okay Jalon replied. Have a good night my sweet kisses on the phone. Good night my love kisses on the phone by replied to Caroline because he was now home parking is car in the garage.

The Rehearsal

It was the day before the wedding and all the guests and family had already arrived in town, and the pastor, wedding coordinator, church attendance, and pianist was waiting at the church awaiting the arrival of the bridal party participants, Jalon and Caroline finally arrived and there was a clap of ovation! Meanwhile two of the bridal party was now late but was on their way. They got lost and finally found their way to the church. As soon as they arrived, the pastor, coordinator, church attendance and organist were in place. The coordinator organized the people in their proper position as the pastor gave directions the rehearsal began the pianist start with the pro-session music for the bridal party March for the bridesmaids, groomsmen then for the flower girl and ring bearer then the maid of honor and the best man the parents of the bride and groom and finally the bride and her groom! As they stood in place and looked at each other. It was emotional, tears of joy for both as the pastor starts to rehearse the vows and their own vows, the lighting of the candles, etc. the rehearsal went on without complications. Everything was well, the bride and groom was both happy with smiles and excitement and anticipation and was a bit nervous but very happy. The evening ended and the couples thanked everyone for coming and participating by playing their role in the rehearsal. They all said good night and embraced each other and went their separate ways because the next day would be a long one and they needed to get proper rest for that day.

Jalon, Caroline, and the pastor spoke briefly afterwards to finalize things, they also brought their marriage certificate ahead of time, so they will not forget it on the big day! They both spoke briefly with their coordinator and assistant to finalize any loose ends, and then they both spoke briefly, kissed, and embraced each other for the last time as "singles" then went their separate ways, Caroline caught a ride home with Pam her maid of honor, Pam talked about how magnificent and beautiful. The sanctuary is including the well-manicured property on the outside as they drove home, at this time, Caroline thanked him once again for her surprise bridal shower. Then she replied. Once again, that is what a friend is for! Then Caroline asked her so "how was your date"? she replied, it was okay! Re is a looker but he is not the one. That is all she said there because she did not want to go into detail, then Caroline is sorry to hear that you do not be dismayed the right one is out there somewhere waiting for you is just a matter of time. Pam dropped Caroline home kissed and embraced her good night, let me know you ladies in safely Caroline ask Pam, okay she replied. As soon as I get in, I will text you, sounds great Caroline replied. I will be waiting. And Pam droves away. As usual, as soon as Jalon arrived home, he called Caroline. They spoke briefly then said good night. quickly fed and took Dexter for a short walk outside afterwards she was off to bed! Her mind was racing the excitement of tomorrow and she was a bit nervous. She was thinking about the time she must be awaken in the morning, she set her alarm and attempted to sleep but thoughts of her being Jalon's wife was running through her mind and what tomorrow will bring, she cried more tears of joy and finally she fell into a slumber.

"The best thing to hold onto in
life is each other."
Audrey Hepburn

CHAPTER 19
THEIR SPECIAL DAY

Early the next morning, Caroline was awakened by her alarm clock and the birds chirping, it was a beautiful morning. She anticipated the sun had already risen high in the sky! She got up and took a quick shower, got dressed, made a quick cup of coffee, toast, sausage, and eggs for breakfast, anticipating it would be a long day, and may not have the opportunity to eat. She was now excited and a bit nervous because it was the BIG DAY! She let Dexter out for his walk and fed him prior to her leaving home, because she knew it would be a long day and may not get the chance again to attend to him until later that day. Once Caroline was finished, she quickly rushed off to the beauty salon where the bridal party were waiting and getting their hair, nails and makeup done. They were all waiting for her arrival, the cricket attended to her as soon as she got in and sat down, everyone was happy to see her and was very excited for her. Congratulations! They exclaimed and gave her hugs and kisses.

Likewise, Jalon was up early that morning and on his way. He grabbed a quick bite on his way to the barbershop where he met up with the guys, he was a bit nervous at this time but also happy. Upon arrival he was congratulated by friends and some family members and the operators of the barbershop! They attended to him immediately and some asked the question" are you nervous yet? YES! Just a little, he replied as they escorted him to the chair and started his haircut and then shaved him. The barbershop and the beauty shop were well staffed that morning for the bridal party. The group of women so they were serviced quickly as they were to the men. The hours were slipping by extremely fast, and they must hurry because it was noon, and the wedding ceremony started at 3 PM sharp! And vote Caroline and Jalon never liked to be late for anything especially for their wedding.

Now, Caroline was finally finished "you look amazing" the girls said to her, this is your last day as a single woman! How do you feel they ask? Then she replied yes, I know this is the last day, I feel great! I'm excited and now nervous. Likewise, Jalon's and best man teased him and asked him, how do you feel? This is your last day as a single man. He answered jokingly laughing and spoke! I feel great! No more lonely nights and looking for dates, they laughed at him and teased him a little more, most of them said Yes! I do agree. Shortly after the girls were finished too and it was a little after 12 noon and they hurried out of the beauty salon and followed Caroline home, which was where they all gathered to get dressed and picked up. Likewise, the men will get dressed and picked up at Jalon's house.

As soon as Caroline reached home, she offered a quick snack and refreshment for everyone, and everyone sat and relaxed a while because they were basically ready to go except to get dressed. She put some soothing, relaxing music on for the occasion, she excused herself and attended quickly to Dexter and afterwards she joined the girls. Not long after she received a phone call from her son, reassuring her he was okay and that he would meet her at the church on time. Congratulations! Once again mom he replied, thank you Samuel! I am okay, just a bit nervous now, but happy. "That is good he replied that is great! I am so happy for you, I believe you have met your soul mate, your boas." Thanks again soon she replied! Then he said God's blessings be with you both. Thanks again son. Thanks again you would not know how much those words mean to me! I love you Samuel, I love you too mom! As she shed tears of joy, comfort, and affirmation, I will see you very soon. I must go now! Okay he said, goodbye.

Jalon and Caroline had not spoken to each other that morning, just a short text message to each other proclaiming their love and that they could hardly wait to see each other later. At the time ticks away and get closer for pickup they all started to get dressed and ready, the bride's maid got dressed quickly and added their beautiful accessories, while Pam Caroline's maid of honor attended to Caroline with the assistance of another bridesmaid. They surprised to Caroline with the old adage "something new, something blue and something borrowed" they brought her a special accessory that matched her dress, it's beautiful and they placed the earrings, necklace to and bracelet on her, she paused for a moment and then" she said thank you all! And by the way you are all looking beautiful. these are beautiful and matched my dress perfectly" and she shed a few more tears. Pam comforted her and wiped away her tears. As she looked at Pam all dolled up and the other bride's maid, she finally realized that her big day was here, and this is it! And all the months of planning are finally over. As she started getting dressed the doorbell rang. It was the photo and video Graper, they answered the door and let them in, hello they exclaimed, and good afternoon! Good afternoon everyone said and return, Caroline is getting dressed she will be ready shortly, you may have a seat or do what you do best one of the bridesmaids says. While they were waiting for Caroline to be ready, they requested to start video graphing and photographing the bridesmaid that was ready and waiting.

They helped her with her Dress slip and bra then finally her wedding gown, they were all amazed once she put her down on, oh my God they said! You look stunning, sophisticated, and elegant. And the others came out to look at her when she was finally dressed, they said the same! Pam says" Jalon hearts will be racing when he sees you and will be hoping the preacher will hurry up with the ceremony." They all laughed and chuckled. The photography and video graphics came in and started taking pictures and videotaping Caroline. The doorbell rang and it was the florist delivering the flowers, boutonnieres, and bouquets, now everything was complete for the perfect pictures, which was the last thing they were waiting on except the limousines, and they should be arriving in half an hour. Everyone was ready on time and now Caroline is getting a bit anxious as she waits and paces the floor. She took a few pictures and then they gathered together and took more pictures inside and out afterword is she tries to relax.

The girls danced to the music that was playing to lighten up the atmosphere! At the church. The place was already set up, decorated and ready to go. The florist finally arrived at Jalon's home and dropped off their corsages for the men they quickly put them on, because the limousine was on its way to pick them up. As the guest, friends and family starts to arrive, they were received and greeted at the door and were escorted to their seats, some stayed outside and overlook the beautiful, lush landscape of the property and the amazing scenery that overlooks the ocean, as the fresh breeze and beautiful waves arrived ashore off the ocean. The beautiful, tranquil setting sets the mood and atmosphere for such a lovely occasion and day for a wedding. The pastor now arrived, the coordinators, church assistance, pianists was waiting on the arrival before they do anything. His best man and his dad helped him with corsage and tie. As the guest continued to arrive at the sanctuary. They were amazed with the magnificent scenery of the well-manicured landscaping of the property, followed by him the beautiful architectural design of the church.

As they entered the sanctuary the stained-glass windows reflected by the rays of the sunlight bounces off the Windows. The beautiful mahogany wood finish of the pews and chairs, podium with the recessed lightings the Cathedral ceilings and the beautiful chandeliers at the entrance of the Foyer and the column at the entrance. The beautiful floral arrangements by the entrance of the door, each pew, chair and at the altar, there were two Ivory eternity candles & candlesticks. The place was beautiful; their guest was in awe! Wondering how they found such a beautiful place. The limousine finally arrived and picked up the groom and the man on time, now everyone was in their place seated, the pianist and all. The church assistants and attendants signaled everyone on the outside to come in because they were on their way! Now it was time and the limousine was on its way to pick up the bride and the bride's maid, when the limousine arrived at the door they rang the doorbell Caroline was expecting one, but instead it was two cars, one was for the bride's maid and the other a special Rolls-Royce for Caroline and Pam, her maid of honor, she was very nervous, but happy with tears in her eyes. She knew Jalon added that especially for her, she was lost for words as panelists did her and dried her tears. As the driver and Pam assisted her to the car, it was beautiful. Pam was lost for words too; all she could say was OH Wow! And they were on their way to the church. Pam called the pastor and told him they were on their way.

Jalon and his men just arrived, and the guest applauded their entrance as the pastor pulled him aside and whispered in is ears, she is on her way! He smiled and looked around at the beautiful sight and the decor of the sanctuary and the faces of his guests, friends and family smiling at him. He was certainly nervous, but also excited. As the pastor had them prepared and ready in place. The first limo zine arrived with the bridesmaid, and the coordinator and church attendance lined and peered at them outside the foyer before the entrance of the sanctuary door which is now closed. Then 10 minutes later, the bride, to be Caroline, arrived. They escorted her to a special area for her not to be seen by anyone prior to her entrance into the sanctuary. Pam carefully attended to her, holding her bouquet, and assisting her with her dress to prevent wrinkles and spots, she was nervous! Yet happy and Jalon also. She quickly assisted her with her veil to cover her face and the pianist starts to play the entrance music for the parents of the groom entered and sat on the left side front pew, then the entrance of the bride parents, which at this time was Caroline's mom her dad was already deceased, and her son standing in to give her away. Her mom sat on the right-side front pew, then entrance of the bridesmaid and the groomsmen as they walked in the guest, family and friends was in awe of how beautiful and elegant they looked, they were all taking pictures smiling and talking, Caroline's son finally arrived he made a wrong turn and got lost. He met with her in the special room and embraced and kissed his mom. He told her how beautiful she looked, he cried, looking at her magnificent face, they were now ready. The groom and his best man were already standing in place and the pastor, the beautiful bridesmaid and groomsmen entered and stand in their place. It was a sight to see the guests. family and friends were in awe once again. Then the entrance of the ring bearer, followed by the flower girl's their entranced as two beautiful twin girls aged seven, entered the sanctuary dropping red petals after they rolled out the white carpet, they were now finally ready for the grand entrance of the beautiful Bride Caroline.

As the pianists start to play her marching entrance song all the guests, family, and friends stand in anticipation of her entrance, snapping pictures of everyone as they arrived. The video and camera man were in place. Nothing missing, not a moment of their special occasion as they made the final moments of perfection with her head peace, and her son at her right side, holding her arm, they stood at the entrance of the door while her maid of honor. Pam handed over her bouquet; the colors were simply beautiful. and magnificent. As she stood behind her, fixing and adjusting the train of her dress, the attendants finally opened the double doors, and the guests were astonished as she entered the sanctuary. The sunrays from the stained-glass windows reflected off the stones in her gown sparkled and glowed as if she was an angel. They were all in awe, and she stood at the altar and Jalon looked at her, he himself was in awe and shed a tear or two. As he came to the beautiful sight in front of him, her son held her by the arm as the guest whispers in awe and astonishment.

The pastor told the people to settle down, so he can start the ceremony. He prayed and blessed the couple, then as he proposed the question "who gives this woman to be wed?" her son Samuel replied, "I do! And as he said that he put her hand into Jalon's hands and quickly stepped aside and sat down next to his wife, son Samuel Jr and grandmother. Her maid of honor stepped into place and took her bouquet and Jalon smiled and took his place. He looked her in the face through the thin veil and held her hands tightly facing the pastor. And they held hands so they could hear the guests whispering how beautiful they looked and how much they admired Caroline's beautiful gown.

The color of her gown was ivory, it was elegantly designed with diamond accented stones, embedded in the uneven shoulder straps, and widely scattered throughout her gown, it was closely fitted from the chest to her waist and from her waist to her knees it was close fit and flared from the knees to her ankles with the beautiful diamond accented stones embedded in the extended train on the back. As Jalon squeezed her hands, he could not wait to tell her how elegant and exquisite she looked. Once again, the pastor gently says to the congregation to settle down so he can continue with their vows! He reminded them that marriage should not be entered into lightly, and that a man should forsake his mother and father and cling to his wife! He also reminded them of the reason and purpose why the Lord gave a woman to man as a gift. Then he went to the Scripture in Genesis that says, "it is not good that that man should be alone, and this is the reason why God gave a woman to a man as his help mate." As the pastor continued and said to Jalon, I do believe you have found your "EVE" your help mate. That is why we are standing here today. After he said that there was a standing operation from their guest!

Then shortly after he continued as he completed his portion of the sermon. Both Jalon and Caroline wrote their own vows to each other. Then the pastor said Jalon" do you take this woman Caroline to be your wife" and he says yes, I do! Then he pulled out the script he wrote to Caroline and said" I will cherish you as the gifts God gave to man, that special price less gift and Oracle God gave to me, I will treat you the best I know how and when I am on sure I will ask him my father for guidance to show me how, how to love and care for you". And as he ended his statement the pastor took the rings from the ring bearer and blessed them and Jalon took Caroline's ring from his hand and placed it on her left ring finger, she smiled with tears in her eyes. Then the pastor continues and said, Caroline "do you take this man Jalon to be your husband "and she said yes, I do! As she read the script she wrote, "I also will cherish and respect you, love and comfort you! And trust you to help guide me and us into God's perfect will for our lives, and when I am unsure how to treat you. I will consult the Lord to guide me." As she ended the statements the pastor handed her the ring, and she took it and placed it on Jalon's left ring finger. He smiled as he wiped away the tears from his eyes with his handkerchief in his pocket. The pastor declared "you are now, husband and wife you may kiss your bride." And there was great applaud from the guests, family, and friends. He hurried and lifted up the veil towards the back of her shoulders and reached out and held her close and passionately kissed her. He then whispered, "you look exquisitely beautiful" and she said thanks you! You look awesome and handsome yourself, then shortly after the pastor read another Scripture and they held hands and tell walk towards the eternity candles and lit them, signifying that they are now united as one.

After lighting the candles Jalon, proudly held is wife then the pastor then pronounces them as Mr. and Mrs. Jalon Victorians. And then they signed their wedding certificate, and their guest gave them another standing ovation and whistled and took more pictures. Then the bridal party formed a line down the middle of the aisle, leading to exit the door as they walked in the center and kissed each other as they entered through the door. As they entered outside an attendant guided them towards the side by the edge overlooking the ocean where there were eight white doves in a cage to be opened and released by the couple. They opened the door releasing the doubts, signifying their new beginning together. It was a magnificent sight to see. They stood around after a while shaking hands and taking pictures with their guest. family and friends. Shortly after the limousine arrived and was waiting to take them to take them to a special place for more pictures while the guest, friends and family stood by and talked a short while and observed the beautiful site by the edge of the ocean and then head towards the reception hall.

Now Jalon's and Caroline were finally alone privately to talk and held and kissed each other, they were in the Rolls-Royce he surprised her with, "what a surprise she, said this is beautiful. I was not expecting this but knowing the type of man you are you; you have wonderful taste and to as I can see you love to give me the best.

Thank you. I appreciate you and I am now happy that you are my husband. I love you! And she hugged him and gave him a delicious kiss. Then he said, "You are welcome! Wow! What a kiss! That was great! Is that an appetizer for later? They both smiled and laughed aloud. Then she whispered" I will not spoil the surprise, let the desert be for later." The bridal group paired up in the larger limousine, Pam, and the best man Joseph, got acquainted by talking a bit for the first time they met was on the night of the rehearsal. But things looked much different now that they were dressed up and socializing!

He complimented her to the gentleman on how beautiful she looked, and she did the same. They will both be happy for their friends. As they continued to talk about them and the circumstances in which they met, that now had a beautiful ending. As the guests arrived at the reception hall, they parked their cars and arrived downstairs that led to the ground they walked down the stairway elegantly designed with mahogany wood encasing and marble floors in Ivory and the beautiful chandelier as they entered the foyer area. As they entered the door leading to the hall they were escorted into a lavishly decorated ballroom and were escorted to their tables. The music was playing to set the mood as they were served refreshments and 'oeuvres' as soon as they arrived.

As they waited to be served, they were amazed with the elegance and beautiful taste they had in choosing such a place as this. As they looked around the room. It was exquisitely decorated to their specifications. The marble floors, the same theme of mahogany wood encasing in the ceiling in a circular shape that looks like a fan and in the center was a large beautiful crystal chandelier, encased in the wood beams was recessed lighting, the area's between the wood beams were clear glass in the ceiling that open up to a skylight, it was beautiful and the windows was elongated windows dressed with beautiful drapes and curtains to match the tiles the tables and chairs was decorated with their colors, coral, ivory and lavender.

Coral tablecloth, ivory chair covers, and chair sashes nicely designed for each chair. The tables were decorated with an elegantly designed long, slender crystal glass vases, encased with multi-colored flowers with glass casing to accentuate the candles around the vase. The dinner plates and utensils were strategically placed, and the glass was decorated with napkins elegantly folded in them. The cake table was lavishly decorated, it was a three-tier cake, the topper was the groom holding his bride in his arms. Ivory colored icing while the flowers were both coral and lavender. And the center dripping on the cake was coral. The table was decorated and has insinuated with candles, draping's and diamond stones that reflects the candlelight.

The dance floor was beautiful. A mahogany-colored wood to prevent slipping during dancing, all the guests were quite content with the refreshments and as they await the arrival of the bride and groom. Finally, not long after, they announce the bridal party and then not long after they announces arrival of the bride and groom. But as everyone waited and look towards the door, they anticipated entering through there was a special entrance only for the bridal party they opened those doors and they announce the arrival of the bridal party, flower girl and the ring bearer flower girl wore coral short-sleeved dress and white shoes the ring bearer wore ivory suite with coral vest and tie and white shoes to match. In the entrance of the bridesmaid and groomsmen coordinated with their colors same as the flower girl and ring bearer. Except for Pam the maid of honor and Joseph the best man. He was extravagant and sharp. He wore an ivory double-breasted suit with lavender vest and tie and white shoes to match Pam's Lavender gown.

Now the entrance of Mr. and Mrs. Jalon Victorians. As they walked down the beautiful mahogany encased spiral staircase and the ivory marble tiled floor, they all stood up to see and took pictures of their entrance into the room Wow! What a beautiful couple the guests whispered! They held hands tightly as they walked into the room, Jalon proudly wore a double-breasted ivory suit and vest and silk shirt and tie and shoes to match. They both said and they arrived in Wow! Look at the decor the exclaimed the coordinator exceeded my expectations of how elegant the place looked as they entered, they were escorted and seated at their tables and were served refreshments as soon as they were seated.

Diner & Toast

Now they were ready to serve the main course, and the pastor bless the food, a short while after they started to serve the main course and the music was just right for the mood, they played soothing dinner music while they ate to relax their souls. They served them first and then the guests! The food was great there was whispered all around the and compliments on their choices, shortly after they had that toast from the best man Joseph, wishing the couple all the very best on their future endeavors and life together. Then, Pam the maid of honor brought a tearful toast about her friend Caroline and what circumstances had brought them together and they became friends. She wished nothing but the best for the future in their lives and blessed their union. The guests applauded after she spoke, and tears of joy ran down their faces as she spoke about the painful past in how they met and how we could have lost her. Then her son made a short speech about his mom, who is the love of his life and a tearful one on the circumstances that Drew Jalon and Caroline together who are now, husband and wife and how thankful he is to the Lord for saving her life for this happy moment. Jalon dad stood up and spoke for a brief moment about his son, how brave and kindhearted he is. There was not a dry eye in the hall.

Their Dance

Then Jalon stood up and thanked his guests, family, and friends for coming and making the day special, he appreciates all of your gifts and sentiments on behalf of himself and his new wife. It was now time for the dance, Caroline stood up and danced with her son and finally had a chance to kiss her grandson. After the dance with her son, he passed her over to her husband, who took over the floor and joined her on the dance floor as they danced to their favorite song. Then after words the bridal party joined in and then Pam and Joseph danced and socialized on the dance floor. She laughed as Joseph told jokes.

Cutting of the Cake

It was now time for the cutting of the wedding cake, as they stood up together Jalon stood behind Caroline holding her hand with her leading for the first slice of cake together, it was romantic as the Fed each other from the first slice of cake, followed by the bouquet toss and removing and tossing the garter. Now the guests who were the lucky recipients to catch the bouquet and garter! YES! Of course, it was Pam and Joseph. Everyone laughed because Joseph was a natural comedian, one who made everyone laugh and made the evening more fun. After the bouquet toss and the clutter placement, they had a surprise raffle to give away those beautiful centerpieces that were on their tables. It was fun.

Everyone hoped and wished their number would be called because they were exquisite vases uniquely designed. Everyone had fun dancing, talking, and laughing the evening away. It was now getting late, the night far spent. As they continued a little while more with their family, friends and guests, as they continued to dance the moon and stars shine through the skylight it was romantic as if they were outside dancing under the stars as Jalon held is why the tightly around her waist and embraced and kissed her, he told her once again how elegant, sophisticated and beautiful she looked and how happy he is to have a such a wonderful and beautiful woman to be his wife. He was so proud of her, Caroline also expressed the same as she held him tight, they discussed once again how the coordinator surpasses their expectations on the beautiful work. She did, they were both pleased and their guests too.

Departure

Caroline whispered to Jalon's that she was a bit exhausted! How about you? She asked, he stated yes! So, they both Jalon and Caroline went to the Master of Ceremony to get their guests attention, they took the microphone and announced their gratefulness and thanked and greeted their family, friends and guests and said good night as they are gracefully departed! But they wanted everyone to stay and enjoy themselves until they were ready to go!

Shortly after they followed them towards the door as they were going into the limousine. They threw confetti and said goodbye! The night was over for them, but most of their get stayed a while longer and danced the night away, talking, laughing and some were singing. Caroline was able to kiss and held her grandson Samuel Jr, daughter-in- law, and son before she left. They were picked up by the limousine and headed home. Home was now Jalon's house. He picked his wife up out of the limousine and walked upstairs toward their master bedroom. It was beautifully decorated for their special night as he walked with her in his arms towards the bedroom. Caroline was amazed, she was in awe, more surprises. She spoke! She was now lost for words! Jalon, did you do this she asked? Yes! he answered! You are such a romantic man! I love it, she said, rose petals was everywhere from the front entrance of the door leading to their master bedroom the rose petals were her colors, Candle lights, soft, romantic music was playing in the background and a bottle of red wine and champagne was chilling, food and drinks was set aside just in case they had an appetite later...Jalon, gently laid her on the bed and kissed her with a deep and passionate embrace. She was certainly nervous, because this was her first time venturing into his bedroom, she passed by and viewed it in the past while she visited, but this was the first official visit into the suite. A beautiful white Chase, just like the one she has at home sits in a corner in the sitting area in the master suite, he brought it as a gift, because he wants her to be comfortable and feel at home. And as he kissed her, he held her in his arms tightly, the bath water was already set in the master bathtub and was ready to go, Caroline being the kind of woman she was wanted to be clean and fresh smelling for him. She kissed him, as she walked towards the bathroom that was also filled with fragrant candles and rose petals and in the bathroom was another bottle of red wine sitting by the side of the tab chilled and ready. He slowly unzipped and took off her gown and unhooked her bra, but she held on to it because she was a bit shy seeing this was the first time he would see her naked, he caressed and kissed her lips and neck that was slightly sweaty and salty from the long day, the light from the candles, reflects and exposed her soft silky skin and back as he attempts to pull her slip but she left them on, she quickly unbuttoned his jacket, vest and shirt and removed his tie. She teased and kissed his lips and neck as he hurried pulling and hopping out of his pants tossing it aside. She walked towards the bathroom to freshened up from the long day, as she tries to chase after her, pulling on her slip, pulling her towards him as she walked away, he was still trying to get caught up with her he followed her, she finally removed her slip and bra, wow he said to himself she is beautiful! her beautiful figure. As her silhouette shape from the light of the candles reflects from the wall. Jalon was amazed, excited, and aroused, he hurried into the bathroom and gently pulled her towards him kissing, caressing and fore play by kissing her from her forehead, neck, ears, and lips. She quickly slipped into the bathtub, he quickly joined her and continued to kiss her massaging her breast gently and then kissing her soft silky skin leading to her stomach holding and embracing her gently, gently, he was excited and erected. From there touching her everywhere she wanted pleasure and as their imagination carries them that makes them happy, then he made gentle, passionate love to her consummating their marriage. After making love to her. He held her close still kissing on her, washing her, and massaging her head and whispering sweet nothings in her ears. Shortly after he picked her up out of the tub and took her into the shower kissed her from the back of her neck down to her back 'and beyond, the passion was heightened as she bathed him, and he bathed her. They both make each other happy, he was in dreamland then the lovemaking starts again in the shower, he dried her quickly and picked her up walked towards the bedroom and laid her gently on the bed, where he made passionate love to her throughout the night until twilight, they were both in ecstasy!

"Love is someone to share paradise with."

&

Our happily ever after start here."

Etsy

CHAPTER 20
THEIR HONEYMOON

That That morning they did not rise early, they were still tired and slept in until noon! They arose and ordered a late breakfast because they had a 3 PM flight to catch. Their bags were already packed and ready at the door, so when the cab arrived everything was ready to go. Before they left for their trip. Caroline called her son Samuel, she wanted to give him the keys to the house and to remind him to take care of Dexter! Until they return from their honeymoon. And she wanted to see her grandson Samuel Jr before she left. Because It was going to be a long two weeks away and she wanted to say goodbye and to hold and kissed him. They arrived quickly and chat for a short while, Caroline told her son Samuel that Dexter was at Pam's house She picked him up after the wedding last night and brought him to her home. And she will be dropping him off at 5 pm today! If it is easier, you can stay at my house until I return.

Whatever is best, and easier for you, she said. Then Caroline said, these keys are yours to keep, yes mom! He replied, no! she said, not a set of keys for emergency they are yours for you and your wife and my grandson. The house is the year officially! Wow! What! Okay he replied you mean you are giving us this house. Yes! She replied it is yours! He was speechless, so what his wife. He barely could say Thank you! But they both did and took the keys and hugged and kissed her. Then Caroline said when we returned, I will complete the paperwork and turned it over into your name, Samuel stood in awe! Once again speechless. Neither he nor his wife were expecting this. Thanks mom he replied. Once again and hugged and kissed her with tears in his eyes. His wife could not control but she consoled him, and they consoled each other.

Once they composed themselves Samuel said! Jalon and Mom, you had a beautiful wedding, congratulations! And as he dried his eyes, Caroline replied and said thanks son and his wife agreed by saying the same and shook her ahead. I know you are getting ready to leave, have a safe trip and have a wonderful time and his wife stated the same as they hugged them once again. The cab drove up the driveway and the driver honked the horn, and they embraced each other with kisses and hugs. As she held Little Samuel Jr tightly and kissed him goodbye. Be safe, Samuel replied. Once again have a good trip and an enjoyable time. So, they pulled their luggage to the door and the cab driver came out to help them, Samuel shook Jalon's hand and gave him a hug and his mom too. At the hurried into the cab, Caroline yelled when we get to our destination you will call you and let you know we made it, so you will not Worry! Okay, they said. Sounds great bye as they waved goodbye.

On their way to the airport, Jalon mentioned to Caroline that little Samuel Junior is growing up so fast. Yes! She replied, and my Dexter too! Yes! He replied, how could I have forgotten him, I will certainly miss him while we are away, he will be in good hands until we get back home Caroline said. I agree he will, he says. As they drove to the airport, they reminisced and talked about their wedding, the wedding coordinator over did herself yes! Caroline replied. She certainly did, Jalon replied. She did an absolute wonderful job organizing and coordinating everything! And your pastor and the rest of the Church assistance too he agreed and said yes! They certainly have. Well! By the time we return our pictures and videos will be ready, Caroline said, I cannot wait to see them." They made it to the airport just in time to check in their luggage and to board their flight. This will be about a 7 to 8-hour ride, and they have a lot to talk about and books and movies to occupy their time, they were happy, this was their first vacation and trip together as a couple. They are expecting to see and to do many wonderful things together on their trip. They got seated and settled in, the flight attendant makes them feel very special and serves them drinks and snacks. They offered them first-class seating free they were elated. They felt as though they were Kings and Queens. The flight was a smooth one all the way and they arrived in Tuscany Italy just in time. As soon as they landed, Caroline called her son so he would not worry and so she would not forget to call him, because her mind was focused on having fun and spending time with her new husband Jalon.

A Limousine was waiting to pick them up from the airport to take them to their hotel! The driver greeted them as they walked up to him holding a sign with their names written on it, as he introduced himself, Jalon shook his hand, and Caroline did too as they greeted each other. The driver welcomes them to Tuscany and helps them to sort through the carousel to pick off their luggage's. He pushed their luggage on a trolley to the car and hurried out of the airport before the heavy traffic rush. I hope you had a smooth ride during your flight, and I hope you will have an enjoyable time here, he says, yes, we did! And we certainly hope so and are looking forward to that! They spoke. The drive from the airport was about 45 minutes as they relaxed and enjoyed the scenery from the beautiful countryside going towards their hotel. Caroline asks if it was much further from here? No! He said we are about another 20 minutes away, great she replied, that is not too bad, it was a long flight she replied, and I am tired. Yes, ma'am! He replied. I do understand.

As they got closer to their hotel. It was embedded on a beautiful mountainside overlooking the ocean on the opposite side, this is beautiful Jalon! Caroline said, then he said yes! I knew I saw it and it was recommended that it is a beautiful place for honeymooners and couples on a vacation. Thank God! I did listen, it is proving to be just right, and I wanted to get a place where you and I will be happy, relaxed and have lots of special moments and memories for a long time. As the driver drove about another half mile, he pulled up on what seemed to be a beautiful villa on the edge of the ocean side and a rear view of the exotic mountain side, Caroline was in awe. Once again, the great taste and surprises Jalon has. At the driver pulled up to the beautiful white fence gate secluded villa, there was a butler there to meet them at the house. He stood at the gate as they pulled up to the gate, and as the limousine stopped, he came up and opened the door and introduced himself and said hello! Caroline and Jalon did too! He helped Caroline out of the car by holding her hand and helping her up, then he helped the driver with the bags and luggage's that was in the trunk of the car into the house. As they entered the villa, the lanai or veranda beautiful terra-cotta tile on the floor they were both surprised, especially Caroline it was a beautiful multilevel meditation style home and it was modernized with all the upgraded appliances with two master bedroom suites, in the living room tray ceiling with a fan, wood beam ceiling in the family room and dining room a seating area, two master bathrooms with a heart shaped tub. And a pool and Jacuzzi in the back patio area. The master bedroom was prepared and ready with fragranced candles and rose petals on the bed, wine being chilled on ice and in the dining room. Dinner was prepared for two with roses and candles on the table and soft music playing in the background. The scented candles brought a beautiful fragrance to the entire house that created a relaxing welcoming feel.

It was already late, so the butler served them as they sat down to relax and eat because they were now hungry from the long trip! Jalon blessed the food and thanked the Lord for a safe trip, while they sat at the dining room table, they looked out the windows that had a beautiful panoramic view of the mountainside and the ocean. It was amazingly breathtaking. As they sat down and relaxed and had supper, it was not long after they were served desserts and afterwards relaxed to do something sounds of the ocean, as they relaxed and laid on the chase in the seating area. They were extremely tired but were full and satisfied. After supper they relaxed and held and kissed each other and fell asleep in each get in arms. By the time they woke up. It was after midnight. So, they went upstairs where the bed sheets were already turned down and was waiting for them to get in, the moon was out. It was beautiful as it shines across the ocean. The butler was already gone, not to disturb them he left a note that he would arrive in the morning and prepare breakfast! They finally went to bed, they felt as if they were at home, the bed was very comfortable and relaxing, the sheets, comforters and pillows were the highest thread counts Caroline said. They rested from that short nap! Jalon pulled Caroline closer and held her tightly, kiss and my staunch and caressed her and she did the same too, this led to a passionate lovemaking once again consummating their marriage, leading them into that beautiful heart shaped roman tub to freshen up! They were kind and gentle to each other.

The next morning at about 10 AM the butler arrived and made breakfast as they laid in bed, they could smell the sweet aroma coming from the kitchen. The smell of freshly brewed coffee, bacon, omelets with sweet peppers, onions and with a bit of ham, toast, and fresh squeezed orange. They arose quickly and took a quick shower in the beautiful step-down shower tiled with marble. Caroline said later she would go in the tub to relax after the long day's trip, they hurried and got dressed and went downstairs. Good morning! They said to the butler, "Good morning," he replied to Mr. and Mrs. Victorian! As he pulled out their chairs and served them like kings and queens, the breakfast smelled, and it looked good Jalon stated Yes! It certainly does reply. Caroline then the butler asks. I hope your bed is comfortable and you rest well! Yes, it was very comfortable and yes you rest well! Thank you for asking. You're welcome, the butler says. If there is anything else that I could do to make you more comfortable or feel at home. Please let me know. Thank you. Caroline says.

As breakfast was served, they talked about the agenda for the day! As the butler gave them some great ideas and a list of activities and tours they can do for the day, as they talked, they agreed on the activity. They would like to view that day, which is the local areas and countryside, and historic sites first. The butler knows just where to take them for the tour as they ate and talked. They viewed the sunrise from the horizon and how beautiful the day seemed it would bring, they concluded with breakfast grabbed their cameras and videos, and her purse and they were on their way!

The days went by fast, they saw and visited a lot of sights and brought a lot of souvenirs and took many pictures and videotapes of the beautiful sights, they had a lot of fun! They enjoyed going out in the evening. a few times, but mostly enjoyed the day trips and activities. They remembered their friends and brought some souvenirs. But most of their Items were for keepsake. Artwork that they both love, and pictures. Caroline Mrs. her grandson and Dexter the dog. As she mentioned missing them, Jalon said "you will be home soon. A week has already passed enjoy it." It will not be much longer until you are home! Are you getting homesick? He asked, Yes! She replied, just a bit, but I am enjoying every moment I spend with you, this is a beautiful place you have exquisite taste, and it is certainly a wonderful and great surprise to me. I am certainly enjoying every moment of it because we may not ever visit this part again for a long time.

We have five days left and we have done a lot and visited quite a bit of places in and around the Tuscany area. I do have another surprise up my sleeve! What? She asked! Then Jalon said if I told you, it will not be a surprise, okay! Then she laughed, he said you will find out soon enough is tomorrow okay for you? Certainly, she replied let us head to the Villa, so you. Relax, because tomorrow is going to be an amazing day. As soon as they arrived at the Villa the butler ran her and bathwater in the Jacuzzi tub! Dinner was prepared and ready, the butler warmed it for them while they took a shower and a bath, shortly they were dressed and at the dinner table they ate, they sat outside and talked for the rest of the evening looking at the beautiful ocean waves coming in. Caroline called her son and daughter-in-law to check on their family and the dog Dexter, all was well.

Early the next morning the butler prepared breakfast and then took them to the train station, Jalon had booked a romantic five days' excursion on the bullet train that travels the Italian countryside, from Tuscany Italy, through Rome, Paris France. They had a very nice sized quarter where they slept. It includes breakfast, lunch and dinner and sightseeing as they stop through the different towns and countries. It was romantic. They met many other couples that were doing similar things on their honeymoon and vacation, some of these couples exchanged numbers with a few! As they met new friends and socialized during the evening at dinner, they would use special times in the evening before bed to fellowship and spend time with the Lord before going to bed. Besides, these excursions went by very fast because they were having so much fun and excitement, they went sightseeing, took pictures, videos and shop they had a great time, met new friends!

"This is the one time I will cherish always for the rest of my life." Caroline said I will too Jalon replied, no amount of money can ever have captured this time we spend together here, I agree. Caroline said, this was a great surprise, you have certainly done a good job! And certainly, it has great taste. Thank you! She spoke. The tour was now over, and they were on their way back to Tuscany, they arrived late that night, but the butler was waiting to pick them up and take them to their Villa. It was a short ride from the station, their meal was already prepared and the Jacuzzi for them to freshen up. They were excited, especially Caroline as she talked to the butler from the station and told him about the beautiful excursion they had had. They took their showers and came down for the evening, ate and relaxed inside watching television and then went to bed.

The next day was the last day, and they stayed locally and relaxed. Most of the day at the Villa and they wrestled and chased each other around the house like children, playing on the playground. The butler packed their bags and souvenirs they were ready to go early the next morning to the airport, they turned in early that evening after supper and rose early that morning and got ready to go, the butler had prepared their final breakfast a nice breakfast before they go, they ate and was satisfied. They gave him a handsome tip for a time well spent and well deserved. He put their baggage in the limousine and entered and sat down, held hands, and talked, they were off to the airport. Once again, they arrived on time checked in, hugged, and shook the butler's hand and said thanks for everything, and for treating us kind, he shook their hands and said God be with you as you travel home, have a safe flight goodbye! And they waved goodbye to each other as they walked away. As they entered the plane.

"Our New Beginning" ACG

CHAPTER 21

RETURN TO THE SANCTUARY

It was a couple of hours; it was a long flight, but they landed safely about 8:30 PM that night! They were happy to be home, yet a bit sad because the trip went by so fast, family well her son wanted to pick them up from the airport because he missed his mom and Caroline wanted to see her grandson too! They quickly picked up their bags and luggage's from the carousel in the baggage claims area, Samuel was waiting outside to take them home! He was anxiously awaiting their arrival and exiting the room, his wife held Samuel Jr, they walked towards the door. As they entered. If they saw them coming out, it was like a family reunion, they were so happy to see each other they yelled! Welcome back! We miss you. Glad you made it home safe. I hope, we hope, you had a great time! Then her daughter-in-law Laurie asked "did you have a good trip and a great time? Yes! They replied, "We had a wonderful time, and we missed you! As they talked, they quickly reached out and hugged each other, while Jalon shifted Samuel's hand and embraced and hugged his wife. Caroline gently stretched her arms out and held her grandson, she took him, kissed, and hugged him. They thanked them for coming to pick them up! Then Caroline asks how is my Dexter? Was he a good dog? Ben Laurie, her daughter-in-law answered. "He is a good dog and a very smart one at that he is doing fine, I can tell he misses you too." I will bring him to you tomorrow, I figure you both need to get a good night's rest, without worrying about Dexter, okay. Thank you! That is so thoughtful of you! Caroline replied, "I hope it was not too much to take care of him and the baby! No Mom! As I said he is a good dog.

They packed their luggage and bags in the trunk of the truck and were on their way home, it felt so good to be home. Caroline said it is nothing like home, nothing like your own home even though the Villa felt like home we will get good sleep tonight, just because we will be in our own beds! I agree Jalon replied! Well, I am happy you are both safely home and you had a great time! Her son said. I have a little something for you, but I will give it to you tomorrow when you bring Dexter! Okay! Thank you, they replied. What should have been a long ride seems short because of the excitement and their conversations while they ride home. They made it home and quickly unpacked their bags from the trunk of the car and placed them in the foyer entranceway. Thanks again! to pick us up. Our pleasure, they stated you are welcome! We will not hold you much longer, get some rest, Samuel replied. That was a long trip! Yes, it was Jalon says. Good night! And good night to you both, drive safely going home and they give each other hugs and kisses goodbye. We will talk with you tomorrow; God bless Jalon replied.   They shut the doors of the truck and entered and drove away as soon as they drove away, they locked the front door, Ah! Caroline replied nothing like home and Jalon replied and said not just that, I will have you here with me, I will not be here alone anymore Amen! Then Caroline asks, "Are you hungry? He replied no not very hungry. So, they hurried, and freshened up and changed into something comfortable, held and kissed each other, watched a little television, and then fell asleep.

The next day Samuel called and stopped by around noon because it was Saturday. He did not want to disturb them by coming too early, after he called Caroline, she arose and made breakfast and took a quick shower, she was dressed and ready waiting for Samuel to arrive with Dexter, while she was waiting. She quickly unpacked the gifts she brought for them, not long after there was a knock at the door! She answered the door, and it was Samuel and Dexter. He knew he was home because he was sniffing, barking, and scratching at the door trying to get in. He could not wait; he was so excited and happy wagging his tail. Caroline answered the door and Dexter jumped up on her leg licking her hands, "hello, Dexter she said how are you, my boy! I missed you too as she stooped down hugged and played with him by rubbing his head and belly. HI Samuel, as you can see Dexter greeted me first no problem mom he replied, he missed you! Yes! She said, quite naturally you can tell he did! Then

Samuel said. I said and walked him before we came so you will not have to, thank you Samuel, Caroline replied for keeping him that was so thoughtful of you. So! Good morning how is you today! And hugged him as she was talking, he replied I am doing great! That is good. Caroline replied how are my grandson and Laurie doing? She asked, he answered they are doing well! JR was still sleeping when I left the house. Then she said. Oh yes, about the house Samuel, I will be arranging to pick up some of my personal items in the next week or so, so you and your family can move in. Mom! He said, and gave her a big hug, thank you once again he replied, you are welcome! Do not say another word, which is the least I can do for my only son. As they sat at the table. She asked to have you he him yet. Yes, mom! I did. Then he asked where Jalon was. She answered, he is still in bed, he was still tired from the jet lag of the long flight, It seems that way replied to Samuel.

It was not long after, they heard footsteps coming down the stairs! Good morning Jalon says good morning. Caroline and Samuel replied as she reached over and kissed him. I did not want to disturb you, I hope we did not wake you, No! Jalon replied, it was the sweet-smelling aroma from the breakfasts you made that woke me up! And I got hungry smelling it. So, I decided to get up. Oh, I see! Well see I have already prepared a plate for you. Okay! He replied that it is great! thank you. Enjoy, I will join you. Shortly after, they all sat at the dining room table. They talked about their trip and the guests and family. That was at the wedding. They met at the church service. While they were away. Samuel talked extensively about how beautiful the wedding was, then she picked up the gift bag, on the chair and handed it over to him, what is this he asked, he was curious to know what was in it, thanks mom! He replied.

Open it when you get home, it is for you, Laurie your wife, and my grandson. Dexter ran over and jumped up on Jalon's legs and licked his hands and face, as he hugged and greeted him home, he pots him on the head and continued to eat and gave him a small sample bite of his sausage, he took it and laid on the floor at his feet ate it and looked at him as to say, I want more! Drooling and staring at him. Shortly afterwards Samuel said goodbye to them, I have some errands to run before I get back, okay! They both replied. Jalon shook his hand and said thanks again for keeping Dexter and for all you did at the wedding, you are welcome he said, it was not a problem at all, and his mom kissed and hugged him and said goodbye! Thanks again for the gift, you're welcome! she replied.

As she walked with him to the door, Dexter Followed behind them, Samuel said goodbye Dexter and rubbed his head and then kissed his mom goodbye and went out the door, she waved goodbye and yelled tell your wife I said hello and kissed my grandson for me, we will talk later! As soon as he drove away. She locked the door behind her, she sat down and talked with her husband and finished eating her breakfast," look at Dexter she said he has grown and gained a few pounds since we left "yes! It seems to be, so Jalon replied. And thank you for the breakfasts, honey! You are welcome. It was good. I was hungry, but once I woke up and smelled it cooking. I am happy you enjoyed it, sweetheart, she said, and he gave her a kiss. I am certainly full now! He said, "Now that we are finished eating could you help me unpack the bags, Caroline asks? Jalon said certainly, as they start. To unpack the suitcases and set aside the gift and souvenir! Then Caroline asks for honey! Do you have any plans for today? No! He replied just going to relax and lay around the house for the rest of the day and get caught up on some sports updates and later some studies. Why! What do you have in mind, Jalon asks! She said, nothing really! Do you mind if we have company for a short while? No! Not at all. He replied, "I just wanted to call Pam and let her know we are back and thanked her for keeping Dexter and taking part in our wedding and give her the gifts and souvenirs we brought, I would like to do this, so I will not forget and get too busy! Okay he replied, you will not bother me, as a matter of fact you just reminded me too! I also need to call Joseph and thanked him also and give him the gift we brought him, okay that sounds great, we can kill two birds with one stone. I will call Pam as soon as we are done unpacking, it was not long after they unpacked everything, and the majority were due to be washed and dried cleaned. Caroline got on the phone and called Pam! Hello Pam! We are back home! Pam replied to welcome home! I hope you had a good trip and wonderful time; Caroline says yes! We did. And thank you for keeping Dexter and taking part in our wedding, you looked stunning. Thank you, Pam, replied, you certainly did! Then Caroline asks, "Did you have a good time. Yes! I did, we certainly had a great time, I am so happy to see you made it home safely. Thank you, Pam.,

So how are you? Caroline asks, I am doing ok! just okay she asked! Yes! I would like to see you if you are not too busy today! Then Pam replied actually No! I have no plans for today. I was planning to lay around the house, so this is perfect, I can get out for a while. Okay, Caroline said why don't you stop by so we can talk, that sounds great Pam replied, I will come by in the next hour or so is that good, yes, that is fine. Caroline said. I will see you then! Bye, and they hung up. Then Jalon did the same and called Joseph, but he got his voicemail and left a message, it was now an hour later and there was a knock on the door, it was Pam, Dexter ran to the door and barked, Jalon! Caroline called out, "could you please check and see who was at the door! I will be right out! Not a problem, he yelled as he walked towards the door and looked through the peep hole and yelled its Pam! Please let her in and tell her I will be there shortly, thank you! You're welcome! he yelled. Jalon opened the door, hello Pam! Come in, how are you today, he asked? I am doing fine Pam replied, Caroline will be down shortly. Have a seat and make yourself at home! Thank you she said, hello Dexter she said, as he walked up wagging his tail and laid its head on her lap, as she played with his ears. Then Pam stated and said you have a beautiful home! Thank you he replied would you like something to drink? No thanks, she replied I just had a late lunch! That is good he says.

And how are you, Pam asks? I am doing well He replied, how was your trip, she asked! It was great. He replied, then Pam said I am so happy you both had a wonderful time and a beautiful wedding. Thank you, Jalon, said and for taking part in our wedding, and you look beautiful! Once again, thank you for watching and taking good care of Dexter! She replied, "you are welcome! It was my pleasure what a friend is for. As they talked, Caroline was coming down the stairs, hello Pam, she yelled as she walked towards her excited and happy to see her with her arms stretched out, she embraced her with a big hug and kiss! I am so happy to see you! "I am happy to see you too," Pam said and hugged her tightly, I am so happy to see you are safely back home! Thank God they both replied. And thank you Pam! Then Caroline said we are glad to be home safe thanked God. We have a lot to talk about! So how are you really! I did step away into the sitting room, away from Jalon! Are you okay? Caroline asks once again. Yes! Pam stated, you don't seem very enthusiastic after earlier on the phone and now it's the same what does wrong Caroline ask? is something bothering you? Then she said nothing is wrong that time will not heal she stated, just a bit frustrated and lonely at times! Oh Pam! I see, I do understand, I believe that will change soon. Thank you, Caroline, for being optimistic. What did Pam say, but I would like to hear about your trip? Okay! Caroline's said, it was great! But we can talk about my trip later, I also want to thank you for taking part in our wedding, you look stunning and also taking care of Dexter. Not a bother at all, Pam said, he is a good dog you trained him well. Thanks. Caroline replied.

Now, back to you, Caroline said! Pam, I am your friend, when you hurt. I hurt too, let us talk! You mentioned frustration and loneliness! Yes! Do you remember that friend and date you met at the restaurant prior to the wedding! Yes! Caroline answered at handsome young man! How could I forget, I thought it would be something, but it turned out to be nothing Pam said! You went out once more after that, but it fizzled out! Okay, I see, I am so sorry to hear about that Caroline said, but Pam be encouraged and do not give up on relationships he probably wasn't the one for you, God has the right one out there for you! I know it sounds easy, because I am now married, but yours is on the way. The Lord is pruning him and pruning you too in certain areas of your lives to complement each other when the time is right! Ooh! Caroline that is sweet I never see, nor thought of it like that before. Thank you for giving me a new perspective on how to look at things now, Pam stated. That is great! Caroline said, and Pam said! I feel much better now, that is why I enjoy talking with you, someone who is always so positive and has lots of wisdom. Then Caroline said that is all God not to me. Are she stated.

Then Caroline said, "I have something for you! For me? Pam asks, yes! You, Caroline, said this will make you feel a bit better; she got up and brought a beautiful bag with a gift in it, what is it! She asked? With a surprised look on her face, open it and you will see Caroline stated, oh thank you! Pam said, you did not have to do this! it is what we wanted to do, Caroline says. She finally opened it, and it was an 8 x 10 painting of the Tuscany countryside. It is beautiful!

Pam replied. She still had that surprised look on her face. Then she continued and said I will cherish it always. Thank you! And gave her a hug as they continued to talk now about her trip! Shortly after Jalon received a call from Joseph and he was coming to visit in another hour, then Caroline received a call from her son and daughter-in-law, thanking them for the gift, it was a set of China from Italy and clothing for the baby. Caroline remembered she also had a few gifts to open too, but she used and shook his hand the time talking and encouraging Pam.

Be in expectation Caroline said to Pam, it will not be long! I hope not Pam replied, and thanks again for being a trusted and true friend. It was not long after Pam said goodbye and was walking out the door while Joseph was walking in, hello! Pam said and greeted him with a warm smile and shook his hand and he replied and said the same and greeted her. How are you? Joseph asks! I am good she replied, thank you for asking. Then Pam said how about yourself! He stated he was doing well and thank you for asking, it was great seeing you again after the wedding. It was good seeing you too, Pam replied, have a good evening! You do the same, he replied. As he stared at her as she walked toward her car and waved goodbye. Caroline was observant but stayed silent. Hello Joseph Caroline said it is good to see you! Come on in! It is good to see you too Joseph replied, "I hope you had a good time on your trip, and I am happy to see you made it home safely. Thank you, it was great, we had a wonderful time, Caroline said and gave him a hug. Jalon is in the family room watching TV! Follow me! Would you like something to drink? No! He replied I just had it early dinner.

Jalon! Joseph is here, it is good to see you, welcome back Joseph said and shook his hand and hugged him. It is good to see you too, Jalon said. Joseph sat down and talked with his friend for a while and watched TV and enjoyed the sports and got caught up with all he missed during his honeymoon. They were excited about their team. How was your trip? Joseph asks! You and the break, It was great! The countryside was beautiful, and the scenery was amazing and the tour we took on the train was awesome. I really enjoyed myself. That is wonderful, Joseph replied. As they continued talking and enjoying the game Joseph stayed about two hours before he decided to leave, well I must go now. It was good seeing you return safely. Thank you! Jalon said. Then Joseph said that was one of the best weddings I have ever attended, everything was well organized, and it was great, including the food. And by the way you looked astounding! You look awesome yourself. Caroline said, and he laughed and said thanks! Thank you, Joseph! They both replied, "We are happy you enjoyed yourself and thank you for taking part in the wedding. You are welcome! It was my pleasure to be a part of the wedding. I would not have missed it for the world! Oh! I almost forgot Jalon said we brought you something when we were away, just a small token of appreciation and love... You did not have to! But we wanted to Caroline said. Joseph looked surprised, then Caroline went to and picked up the small gift that was neatly wrapped and gave it to Joseph. Thank you! He replied, as he in anticipation wondered what was in the package.

He was now curious; he could not wait until he got home to open it! he could not wait until he got home to open it! He quickly pulled off the wrapping paper off the box and opened it, it was one of his favorite colors "Red" and it was a read something on till he pulled it out of the box, it was a Jersey Sports shirt! from one of his favorite sports teams.' This is great. He said thank you and responded with a hug, I must go home and try it on, thank you! You are welcome! Jalon replied and walked with him to the door, once again, thanks. We will talk later, and he went to his car and drove off! As he drove away, he honked his horn and waved goodbye. The evening ended with them talking, relaxing, and thanking the Lord for a good time and bringing them back safely home. Caroline opened a few gifts that she received for their wedding and made a note of who to send thank you cards to; this was their first actual day they were spending together in their home! As a couple, they sat and relaxed, held each other and watched a movie. Dexter was in the midst of them laying at their feet on the floor, he was happy they were home.

The next day was Sunday, but Jalon did not have to prepare any messages till the following Sunday, but they both went into service. The congregation was happy to see them and welcome them back. The weekend went by quickly and the week started with Caroline receiving a call from the video graph and photograph ready to stop by and deliver their pictures and videos. She was excited and could hardly wait until they arrived, they arrived about noon, she was excited to see the pictures and was glad to see the beautiful professional handiwork. She could not wait until Jalon got home to show him the pictures and we watched the videos together. She had the rest of the afternoon to do so. As soon as he arrived home while he was resting, they looked at the pictures and watched the videos and made a decision on which of the pictures to send out with a thank you card to the family, friends and guests. They opened a few more get that was left together and she started to mail out the thank you cards. Once the pictures they have chosen are returned. They were enjoying the house that has now become a home! And enjoying each other as a married couple. As a wife a first lady and as a husband and a pastor.

That Sunday they returned to the church, the congregation welcome them and was happy to see them, it was now eight weeks later Pam was at the mall shopping and she was hungry from walking around the mall, so she decided to stop and grab a bite to eat at one of the local eateries in the mall, as she ordered and sat down to eat. She saw someone in the line waiting to be served that looked familiar. But from behind she was not very sure of who she thought she saw, so she waited until they ordered and attain s a seat, she was right. It was the person she thought it was after all. It was Joseph so she waved at him and called his name, he was alone and was heading in the opposite direction for a seat! When she called his name. He turned around and looked. To his surprise it was Pam. He went over to her and said hello and asked if the seat was vacant, and available she said yes! He sat down and they ate together and talked to, so! He said are you alone, yes, Pam replied, what about you, she asked Joseph replied yes, I am alone. So, to make conversation so you are just out shopping for the afternoon. I see! Joseph asked Yes, Pam replied. I had nothing else to do so I decided to get out of the house, same here. Joseph replied. Pam really did not have much to say except to talk about the wedding and how nice he looked, and Joseph said the same about her, so are you involved? Joseph asked. Then he said I hope I am not getting too personal! No! She replied, "How about you! she asked? No! He replied with a smile on his face. How about a family to be direct children? Pam replied no! Children are just single, and free. Wow! Such a beautiful woman as yourself? I hope I am not being too forward; we will be No! not at all. She smiled and was happy he was asking those questions.

They chat for an hour not realizing the time had gone by so fast, and they stayed a while longer to finish up their meal, it was nice to see you once again Pam said, same here Joseph replied and thank you for inviting me over at your table, you are welcome! Pam said and gave him a hug and said goodbye. She continued to shop and shortly after she received a call from Caroline, who was excited about the pictures and videos, she told Pam that she must come over when she had a chance to see them, that is, ok! Great Pam replied. Certainly! I cannot wait. Then she said it is amazing! Then Caroline asks what the meeting Pam replied and said I was at the mall and surprisingly ran into Joseph! That is good, Caroline replied and told her the details of their meeting, which is wonderful. Caroline said, perhaps it could be the start of something good. Did you exchange numbers, Caroline asked? No! I left it alone, but I enjoyed talking with him... Then Caroline said Well! If something is meant to be. It will come back around. It seems as if he enjoyed Conversa ting with me too! She stated Caroline.

A week later, Pam was at the park exercising and walking her dog. Once again guess who? It was Joseph doing his routine exercise also she ran into him at the were about to pass by each other, WOW! hello again Pam, he says, "This is too much of a coincidence," he replied! How are you today? She replied and said I am doing fine, and she asked the same of him. What a surprise. She said they have met again twice in two weeks, yes! I realized that Joseph said what a surprise! Then he continued and said we need to talk! Would you mind? He asked? She said No! it is okay! He asked, "would you mind if I give you my phone number? Not a problem, she replied! Thanks! And the exchanged numbers. She smiled and was very excited within our heart, we will talk soon, let me finish my exercise, I understand she replied with a smile as she walked away. As Pam walked and did her exercises, she thought to herself "is this for real, It seems too good to be true." She actually pinched herself just to make sure she was not dreaming, and it was reality. She laughed to herself.

As Joseph exercise he thought to himself and said the same "is this for real "I cannot believe such a beautiful woman a single and this is the third time we ran into each other, as the old cliché says "3" is a charm. I do know the Lord knows what he is doing, he sees the desires of my heart and I believe have heard my prayer and have seen the longing and loneliness, I also believe God hides what belongs to you in his own secret way so no one can see it accept you in its timing! Just as he continued to walk and talk to himself. He wonders if she is the one. And as Pam walks, she also wonders to herself if Joseph is the one and if the Lord has finally answered her prayers. The one that Caroline was talking about and prophesying about! Then she started to talk with the Lord and said, you have seen the dark lonely moments that I have cried with no human male companion to talk to! Please show me and give me answers with signs of confirmation following as time goes by. As they both walked and completed their exercises, they spoke briefly. Then, Joseph said. So! Do you come here often, Pam? And Pam replied and said about three times per week.! Oh! He says. That is great! How about you? She asked. And he said about four times per week. That is awesome! She said. And how long have you been coming here to do your exercises. She asked.! He replied. I have lost count. Seriously. As she stared at him. How about, you He asked. She replied about four years. Then Pam said. That's that is good. That's why you look so great. Thank you, she replied. Then he clarified. That is a compliment, not a come on. Because some men do that. and I wanted to let you know I am not one of those men. I am not hitting on you! I know she, replied. You seem to be respectful man! Thank you, Joseph, replied! Then he asks. Would it be OK if we exchanged phone numbers? YES!! Certainly. Pam replied. Eagerly waiting for him to ask with a smile on her face. Then they exchange phone numbers. and said thank you to each other. Then she said. I will be expecting your call, and he replied. I will call you about 8:00 PM. He says, "Well, it's getting late. It was nice seeing and speaking with you." Pam said, likewise. He replied, "Have a fantastic evening and get home safe!" You as well. Goodbye.

The End

Made in the USA
Columbia, SC
01 November 2024

45141726R00141